MMXVI

THE WHITE REVIEW

EDITORS	BENJAMIN EASTHAM & JACQUES TESTARD
DESIGN, ART DIRECTION	RAY O'MEARA
POETRY EDITOR	J. S. TENNANT
US EDITOR	TYLER CURTIS
ASSOCIATE EDITOR	FRANCESCA WADE
EDITORIAL ASSISTANTS	CASSIE DAVIES, IZABELLA SCOTT
DESIGN ASSISTANTS	THOM SWANN, GABRIELLA VOYIAS
READERS	CARLA MANFREDINO, MADDALENA VATTI
CONTRIBUTING EDITORS	JACOB BROMBERG, LAUREN ELKIN, EMMELINE FRANCIS, ORIT GAT, PATRICK LANGLEY, BELLA MARRIN, DANIEL MEDIN, SAM SOLNICK, EMILY STOKES, HARRY THORNE, KISHANI WIDYARATNA
HONORARY TRUSTEES	MICHAEL AMHERST, DEREK ARMSTRONG, HUGUES DE DIVONNE, SIMON FAN, NIALL HOBHOUSE, CATARINA LEIGH-PEMBERTON, MICHAEL LEUE, AMY POLLNER, CÉCILE DE ROCHEQUAIRIE, EMMANUEL ROMAN, HUBERT TESTARD, MICHEL TESTARD, GORDON VENEKLASEN, DANIELA & RON WILLSON, CAROLINE YOUNGER
BOARD OF TRUSTEES	BENJAMIN EASTHAM, TOM MORRISON-BELL, JACQUES TESTARD

THE WHITE REVIEW IS A REGISTERED CHARITY (NUMBER 1148690)

COVER ART BY MICHAEL WOLF
PRINTED BY PUSH, LONDON
PAPER BY ANTALIS MCNAUGHTON (OLIN CREAM 100GSM, OLIN NATURAL SMOOTH 120GSM)
BESPOKE PAPER MARBLE BY PAYHEMBURY MARBLE PAPERS
TYPESET IN JOYOUS (BLANCHE)

PUBLISHED BY THE WHITE REVIEW, APRIL 2016
EDITION OF 1,800
ISBN No. 978-0-9927562-7-7

COPYRIGHT © THE WHITE REVIEW AND INDIVIDUAL CONTRIBUTORS, 2016.
ALL RIGHTS RESERVED. NO REPRODUCTION, COPY OR TRANSMISSION,
IN WHOLE OR IN PART, MAY BE MADE WITHOUT WRITTEN PERMISSION.

THE WHITE REVIEW, 243 KNIGHTSBRIDGE, LONDON SW7 1DN
WWW.THEWHITEREVIEW.ORG

Supported using public funding by
ARTS COUNCIL
ENGLAND
LOTTERY FUNDED

EDITORIAL

THE POLITICAL and internet activist Eli Pariser coined the term 'Filter Bubble' in 2011 to describe how we have become sheltered from opinions that differ from our own. Pointing the finger at such mechanisms as social media streams and the 'personalised' results delivered by online search engines, he warned that the online experience of news and culture was coming to resemble an echo chamber. Our Twitter and Facebook feeds repeat back to us our own points of view, expressed by others who share them; our browsing history makes it possible for advertisers and news sites to guide us towards other things that its algorithms suggest we 'might like', shielding us from anything that we might *not* like, anything new. We become entrenched in our opinions, unable to understand, enter into dialogue with, or even countenance difference. The polarisation of political perspectives in the United Kingdom, United States, and across Europe seems increasingly to bear out this analysis.

It is our hope that little magazines such as *THE WHITE REVIEW* might in some small way work against this tendency towards intellectual isolation, the withdrawal into what Pariser calls a 'personal ecosystem'. We are privileged to be able to place together radically different things within the pages of a single publication. That is much in evidence in this issue, which juxtaposes the systemic critique of Martin MacInnes with Elizabeth Peyton's emotionally charged still lifes and portraits; a discussion of Cally Spooner's scripted performances against the lyrical experimentalism of Geoffrey G. O'Brien's poetry; Evan Harris's attempts to find the appropriate form for his experience of the failures of British education beside Sophie Seita's investigations into the properties of language. The art critic Orit Gat investigates the tendency towards homogeneity in the way that art is presented on the internet, and calls for a new plurality. We hope that print publications such as ours can offer new and surprising encounters.

Yet, as we have noted in previous editorials, patterns seem to emerge in each issue, though their form might (like clouds) be informed by the reader's own state of mind. The reminiscence prompted by the recent celebration of our fifth birthday might explain why, when reading through the first proofs of this issue, we were struck by the recurrence of memory as a theme across the issue's wide variety of styles. Gary

Indiana, the great writer and filmmaker, talks in an interview of his disdain for our generation's lazy nostalgia for decades past, while considering how it's possible to transform personal experience into literature. Chris Kraus and Alexandra Kleeman explore how time changes our relationship to place, to other people and to ourselves, demonstrating how memory's propensity to mislead can be realised in fiction. In a different register, the philosopher and novelist Tristan Garcia plays upon our notion of cultural inheritance in a story about pop music, plagiarism, and the fallacy of creative inspiration. Lawrence Abu Hamdan – an artist and 'private ear' whose work was submitted as evidence at the UK asylum tribunal, and who has collaborated on legal cases with Defence for Children International – proposed the publication of a verbatim transcription of an interview undertaken by a refugee in application for asylum. The applicant is asked to speak, without pause, for fifteen minutes, so that her accent can be used to identify her. She talks of her childhood, her memories and her formative experiences.

A single issue – in the example above, of the relationship between memory and cultural identity in a rapidly changing world – can be addressed and understood by a plurality of approaches. We share the same concerns, but have different perspectives upon them. We hope that this little magazine might, in its own particular way, remind us to seek out and attempt to engage with styles, forms, and ideas other than those to which we have already declared allegiance.

THE EDITORS

ABSOLUTE LOVE

BY

CHRIS KRAUS

IN THE NORTHERN HEMISPHERE summer or spring of 2011, S., a middle-aged writer was invited to speak at a conference on art in Wellington, New Zealand, Since S. had lived in that city between the ages of 14 and 21, attended its university, and made yearly trips back to visit her parents before they returned to the US when she was in her late thirties, Wellington was where she was considered to be 'from'. S. no longer knew where she was 'from'. S. was then of an age where she thought about age at least eight times a day. Having spent parts of her life in New York and LA, she knew where she was 'from' didn't matter much. When she was a student at Wellington High School, S. recalled being told by the head English teacher, a salt-and-pepper-haired man in baggy black and white tweeds who'd published critical essays on D. H. Lawrence, that because of her emigration from the US at such a formative age, she had no nationality and therefore, despite her interest in literature, could not be a writer. Which is to say, S. had lived through various eras including the demise of nationalism.

From the moment she stepped off the plane (arriving from Melbourne, where she'd attended another, more international conference) S. regretted this trip back to Wellington. The weather was windy and cold, the bleak streets were festooned with banners that said *Absolutely Positively Wellington*, part of a civic re-branding attempt that even her professionally cynical colleagues seemed to find admirable. Except for the weather, the city was almost unrecognisable. Streets had been re-routed to accommodate heavier traffic, and the low, earthquake-prone limestone buildings had mostly been razed and replaced with uniform, steel-reinforced high-rises. The domed structure on Courtenay Place known as the 'Taj Mahal', built in the 1920s as public toilets but used mostly for furtive homosexual cruising and vice squad entrapment, was now a boutique locavore restaurant. Shabby Victorian houses with bed-sitting-rooms let by the week to unmarried secretaries and widowers now sparkled like jewels in the dung, transformed into bright spacious homes for professional families.

Conference attendees were housed at the James Cook Hotel, which S. found very confusing. Built in 1972, backing onto the American embassy building, it had once been the pride of the city, with its sleek glass façade and tube-shaped glass lift that rose to a sweeping view of the harbour. S. had attended dozens of demonstrations outside the hotel, but had only once been inside it, when she interviewed the prime minister's wife for the newspaper's women's pages. The hotel had since been updated as a mid-market family accommodation. Its burgundy carpets and recessed lights lulled her ever more deeply into the numbing cocoon of international travel. *Where was it?*, she thought, *where was the city?* She went out for long walks, couldn't find it. Her co-headliner, L., had flown in with his wife from London two days before. Each time she met L. and his wife in the lift or the hall they were beaming and bright, on their way out to have breakfast or dinner or drinks with their New Zealand colleagues. L. and his wife were more than a decade younger than S. Still, she was impressed and amazed and wondered, *how do they do it?*

The conference was held at an art school built on the grounds of the former Dominion Museum and Wellington High School. It went on for two days about things S. mostly felt did not concern her. Whenever the lights weren't dimmed for a Powerpoint presentation, she stared down at her lap reading a novel. But when S. got onstage to read from her book, she felt herself locked in the gaze of a tall and lean elderly man in the dead-centre seat of the less-than-half-full auditorium. Why was he staring at her? The man had long, scraggly blond hair. He wore Wrangler jeans and a black oilskin parka – a look that was deeply familiar to S., as it comprised the whole wardrobes of most of the anarchist poets, radical activists, graduate students and junior lecturers she met years ago every week in the pub and often slept with.

During the break, she signed books with smiley faces and flowers while the strange-but-familiar old man hovered alone, close by the table. Glancing over the shoulder of whatever young artist or fan she was chatting with, she studied his slightly stooped shoulders, his oval face, his Nordic eyes behind rectangular engineer's glasses. And it was R.! R., the lone potter, who drove into the city most weeks for Friday night shopping, a three-hour frenzy that gripped the whole city each week and ended up in the boozer. For as long as she'd known him, R. lived on a farm that he'd bought in the then-faraway Wairarapa Valley.

R. belonged to a distinguished New Zealand intellectual family, his mother a writer, his father a pedagogical theorist who'd abandoned the family and taught at an American university. R.'s mother prevailed after an ugly divorce, raised her four sons alone and became more and more famous. Younger than R. by a couple of years, R.'s brother D. was a philosophy lecturer at the university. S. slept with D. on a casual basis during her second year as a student, the same year she'd been promoted at her job on the newspaper, until one night, probably drunk, D. smiled at S. while they were fucking and said, *I'm gonna make you pregnant, bitch... then we'll see if you're still a senior journalist.* This shocked her enough to avoid D. in the future.

S. didn't want to get pregnant. Getting pregnant in Wellington entailed the inevitable visit to Dr G., who famously groped his clandestine patients while they were sedated and strapped to the table. Nor did she even especially want to be a reporter. Given a choice, she'd rather have been a philosophy professor like D., or a lost girl, or an actress. She saw no reason for D. to resent her, and his outburst was hurtful. S. had already had her fair share of perfunctory sex, but until now she'd never encountered a hate-fuck.

D.'s brother R., on the other hand, always spoke to her kindly. After the ugly encounter with D., she found ways to be jostled and pushed next to R. on those loud Friday pub nights, as if his recognition could somehow erase the night with his brother that left her flooded with shame whenever she thought about it. R. seemed to welcome these meetings. Whenever they talked, he moved even closer to S. than the Friday night pub-crush required. S. came to see R. as poetic and valiant, his retreat to the country, and work with his hands, as a principled stand against glib intellection. She believed she and R. understood each other. As time went on, S. looked forward to these Friday nights as a chance to see him. The colour drained out of the vomit-beige room on nights when he wasn't there. S. found that she could summon R. up simply by closing her eyes. She heard his voice in her brain, saw his face etched onto her eyelids.

It was well known that R. did not live alone. He shared his farmhouse and kiln with a woman named A., also a potter, who favoured long calico skirts and never came to the city. It was also well known that R.'s arrangement with A. was most likely temporary. F. was his true love. Not much was known about F., except that she was living in London, holding some kind of embassy job (clearly, although not at the time, F., like R., but unlike A., was the child of an upper-middle-class family). F. wrote to R. regularly of her plans to return to New Zealand in a near but indefinite future.

Nevertheless, when R. mumbled a vague invitation for S. to visit the farm, she jumped at it. During the week, phone calls were exchanged. On Saturday morning, S. would hitchhike from Wellington out to R.'s farm, two and a half hours away, and spend the night with him. The next day she'd catch the bus back to the city.

All week she thought about how it would be, what she would wear, what they'd do, what they would say to each other. It would be perfect. It would be some kind of payback, although S. at the time saw it more as *redemption*. That morning she put on a pair of heeled boots, a sweater and jeans and an expensive suede jacket, the kind of outfit she'd wear to a press conference. Luck carried her from the railway station on Waterloo Quay to the Hutt Valley motorway, over the Rimutaka mountains all the way to R.'s farm, all of these rides synchronous and perfectly timed for an appropriate mid-afternoon arrival.

But as soon as she got there, it was awkward. The farmhouse that lay at the end of an unpaved muddy road was unfinished and rustic. R. opened the door and embraced her, but when S. stepped into the room A. was still there, resentfully tossing some things into a flax Maori kit-bag. The two women nodded and smiled. Then A. opened the sliding-glass door to the yard and departed meekly. Clearly, A. and R. had made some prior arrangement; one maybe not much to A.'s liking. This threw S. off-balance, but once she and R. were alone, things settled down. She was nervous, for sure, but the atmosphere stabilised. R. offered to show her the farm and their pottery workshop. He gave S. an old pair of gumboots, probably A.'s, so her feet wouldn't get muddy.

It was a bright, late fall day, thunderclouds racing across the sun, and thankfully night came on quickly. R. heated up a big pot of gruel on the antique wood stove, the kind of gruel everyone ate, made of butcher-bones, bay leaves and lentils. They sat on big cushions eating their gruel out of pottery bowls beside the fire. When R. put on a record they stood up and kissed very slowly. S. remembers the song, The Rolling Stones, 'Angie', and she remembers the kiss: elegant, minimal, musky and sweet like her favourite dessert, pears and black coffee. And then they must have made love, but S. can't remember.

Any future between them beyond that one night was unlikely, as S. must have known from the start. But still, she was devastated. Each night that week, she sat at the desk in her room at the Aro Street flat, writing a letter she hoped would convey her rage, hope and disappointment. Why did she feel so betrayed? She typed it on dozens of sheets of the thin 5x7 copy-paper she used for the newspaper, read it out loud to her flatmates and then rewrote it. S. was 17, maybe 18 years old. She wanted nothing and everything. She can't recall if she sent it.

Eventually, S. left for New York. F. returned from London and within months, she and R. married. Handsomely, guiltily, R. gave A. the farm, although she had no legal rights to it. He and F. purchased another derelict farm just a few miles away, and built a new house on it.

In New York, S. stayed for two weeks with P., R. and D.'s eldest brother, in his Upper West Side apartment. She'd never met P. before, which, among that group of friends at the time, was no reason not to become a long-staying house guest. P. had a glass eye, and attended both group and individual therapy with a messianic figure named Barry. A sociologist at the UN, P. had become, his brothers said, 'completely American', which of course was pejorative. Most likely S. slept with him. Meanwhile back in New Zealand, K., S.'s younger sister, went out briefly with J., R., D. and P.'s youngest brother. Between them, they joked, before K.'s mental breakdown that turned out to be permanent, they'd slept with the entire family!

During one of her many trips back to New Zealand, S. learned from D.'s new wife O. that R. and F. had a haemophiliac baby. *Can you imagine?* O. whispered loudly to her over the music. (The Wellington people S. knew had begun getting married, but hadn't stopped gathering at aimless after-pub parties that routinely wound down around 2 when the same diehards passed out from drinking.) *She knew all along she was carrying haemophiliac genes, but she didn't see fit to tell R. until late in the pregnancy.* O. worked at the Department of Child and Social Services. Dismissed from his university job for having sex with an undergraduate student, D. had taken up furniture-making. *Perhaps mores have changed?* S. wondered briefly. D. and O. commuted between her Wellington flat and his furniture workshop close to R. and F.'s farm. *It's a roll of the dice*, O. continued. *For people who carry this gene, there's a one in three chance that the child will be born haemophiliac.* On her next trip back to New Zealand,

F

S. learned from O. that R. and F.'s second child was also born haemophiliac. *Rilly bad luck, inn't it?*

S. hadn't thought about any of these people for almost two decades. Her new friends or art colleagues in New Zealand were younger, not older than she. They were part of the international circuit. So it wasn't as if the years melted away when she broke off signing books and embraced R. in the auditorium foyer... But, looking into his face as he stood closer-than-normal beside her, just as he had in the pub all those years ago, she felt the same current passing between them, however diluted... a possibility of understanding that could lead to but wouldn't finish with sex, which she'd taken for absolute love thirty years ago.

R.'s two sons were grown. One moved up north, the other lived in Australia. Treatments improved, they survived, still they were struggling. F. had gone back to school and become a psychologist, and they still lived on the same farm in the Wairarapa. A few years ago, R. had begun painting. Considered one of the foremost New Zealand potters, he'd gotten bored with ceramics. He still fired some work to help cover the bills, but his heart wasn't in it. Instead, he'd been commuting to Wellington for the last couple of years, doing a Fine Art Ph.D. at the art school. S.'s new friends were his teachers.

Leaning still closer, they exchanged views of the conference, which were, of course, similar. S. wished she could see some of R.'s paintings. *Listen,* R. said, before they had to go back into the room for the Institutional Critique roundtable, *why don't you come out and visit on your way back to Auckland? You could stay overnight and meet F. D. and O. are still there. D.'s followed your work. I know he'd love to see you.*

S. agreed right away. Skipping cocktails and dinners to take long walks in the city for the next several days, whenever she passed an old coot in an oilskin parka, she asked herself, *Did I fuck him?* She'd just finished Proust, the last book, *Time Regained*, and it was exactly like that... the heroes and villains of her early youth now impossibly aged.

At the end of the week, she drove her rental car to Wairarapa, the treacherous road over the mountains now replaced by a highway. This time, she didn't think much about what lay ahead, but R. and F.'s home was exactly as she might have imagined it: the planked floors and rugs, D.'s handcrafted furniture, tasteful but not overdone, open and comfortable. F. worked three days a week with troubled youth, mostly Maori, their families newly arrived after being priced out of the city. She was warm and professional, cordial. Outside, about a hundred sheep grazed: a flock R. was raising for slaughter and wool, both for income and principle. He was no hippie herder or gentleman farmer.

D. and O. came for dinner: lamb chops, roast kumara, salad. They'd had two children, too, both of them living in Europe. *Ah, ya see?* D. said. *We stayed here. You spend eighteen years raising your kids and they fuck off as soon as possible.* O. had retired. He was still reading and writing philosophy.

Thirty-five of R.'s paintings hung in the woolshed he'd reclaimed as a studio: half-figurative Richter-ish representations of riots and refugee camps rendered from newspaper photos. S. loved the paintings, but as she was praising them, she knew they didn't stand much of a chance in the art world. If R. made the same work but was twenty years younger, had different friends and used different words to describe them, they would be viable. There was a half-finished canvas that featured a lean, intense woman with one arm raised in the foreground. He'd finish that painting for her. S. thought long and hard about how to help R. exhibit his paintings, and after leaving New Zealand she'd try, but her currency didn't extend to such favours.

Tomorrow morning, do you want to drive out to Palliser Bay? R. asked her that night in the studio. Now that the mystery cards had all been revealed whatever energy field was bouncing between them that day at the conference had settled into something calm and familiar. She'd never been to Palliser Bay, a remote stretch of coast accessible only by miles of dirt road, home of the North Island's largest seal colony.

They took two cars to Masterton, parked S.'s rental and bought a disposable camera. From there, they drove about 20 miles in R.'s car, passing few houses or vehicles. It was a bleak winter morning. They got out of the car. Walking a few hundred yards from the road to the rocky coastline, they saw hundreds of grey furry seals and their pups, on rocks and in caves. They climbed over the rocks. Once, R. extended his hand to help her onto a ledge, but R. had a wife and S. had a partner and clearly nothing further than this would happen between them. S. was too old to squeal. Instead, as R. watched her, she tiptoed as close as she dared to the seals and took photos. The outing, while pleasant, was already redundant. She took no pictures of R., he took no pictures of her.

She left the camera with R., who developed and mailed her the photos. Emails and gifts were exchanged, but S. can't recall what became of the photos.

F

INTERVIEW

WITH

ELIZABETH PEYTON

THIS INTERVIEW with Elizabeth Peyton, one of the most celebrated painters of recent times was conducted by Nicholas Cullinan, Director of London's National Portrait Gallery. The two met in 2014 when Cullinan was planning his current exhibition at The Metropolitan Museum of Art, *Unfinished: Thoughts Left Visible*, which included works by Peyton. The art historian first sat for the artist (at her invitation) the same year. If further reasons for inviting the two to talk were needed, we would point to the breadth of their shared interests beyond portraiture: as a curator at The Metropolitan Museum of Art in New York and Tate Modern in London, Cullinan worked on exhibitions by such diverse artists as Tacita Dean, Henri Matisse, Kazimir Malevich, Cy Twombly and Amie Siegel; Peyton's recent exhibition at Sadie Coles HQ, London, featured still lifes, landscapes, portraits and homages to canonical painting alongside linocuts.

The pairing also seems appropriate to Peyton's practice, which combines exceptional technical ability with a sensibility predicated on a sincere emotional connection to her subjects. Her recent work has foregrounded the artist's deep engagement with the history of painting, with inspiration from (and allusions to) Manet, Sargent and Moreau, and seen her practice expand to include pastels and a variety of printing techniques. Her portraits, which have included artists, musicians, and literary, historical and cultural figures, among others, negotiate a delicate line between fidelity to life and self-expression.

———

Q. THE WHITE REVIEW — Your exhibition at Sadie Coles HQ featured not only a range of different genres – portraits, still lifes and landscapes – but also different mediums, from painting to drawing and printmaking. Is this a new direction for your work? Or does it encapsulate what you've been doing before?

A. ELIZABETH PEYTON — I wouldn't say it's a new direction. It seemed important to include the linocuts because a different thing can happen in them than in a painting, it's a different kind of expression. I've been making prints for a long time, monotypes and etchings and the odd woodcut. I like about prints that you have to make it all happen in one go. I don't work on one piece for a long time, an afternoon usually. I tend to try things out. I would say that, historically, prints have typically been the afterword to a work. But for me it's a foreword. Often I'll make a work *after* something I make in the print studio.

Q. THE WHITE REVIEW — Lucian Freud would make a painting of the sitter first, and then afterwards, as a kind of coda or postscript, he would make prints based on the same subject. But for you it's the other way around?

A. ELIZABETH PEYTON — One of the prints at Sadie Coles HQ is of [the musician] Elias Bender Rønnenfelt. When I make work about him, it seems like I've been looking at him for six months, but then we go to the print studio and I make something in two hours. Whereas sometimes I'll try and paint him and really struggle. Even though the print might only have taken two hours, it took all that previous time to get to the point.

I also really want to accomplish something each time I am in the print studio. Sometimes when I'm in the print studio I project my own negative thoughts onto everyone who is working there. When I'm on my own, I sometimes think to myself, 'Why am I painting my dog?

Can't I get it together?' But when I'm printing, I'll scramble to make it happen. Whereas in the studio I might have stepped back from it and let it sit.

Q. THE WHITE REVIEW —— So the limitations of printmaking can, in fact, be liberating?
A. ELIZABETH PEYTON —— I even find myself attempting to replicate that anxiety when I'm painting in order to make myself finish something I've been working on for a long time.

Q. THE WHITE REVIEW —— How does that work in terms of your painting and drawing? When does a painting fail? Do you give up, or do you put it to one side and come back to it later? I don't want to focus on failure, but I think it's interesting to think about the limitations of the medium. Printmaking is a concentrated burst of energy; is it the same with painting?
A. ELIZABETH PEYTON —— No, painting is different. It can be many accumulated quick moments, or happen over a long time, but the difference is that the surface is so important to a painting. In printmaking, the surface is flat. With a painting, the weight of the surface has to be right. It's not about failure so much as it's about letting the painting tell you what it needs. Just watching it, watching everything that's happening in it. A painting takes place over time, so it has many influences coming into it.

Q. THE WHITE REVIEW —— Painting is essentially a process of addition. If something is unfinished, it's because something is lacking or absent. Sculpture and printmaking are processes of subtraction – that's how you get the image, you scrape away or remove.
A. ELIZABETH PEYTON —— Yes, though paintings can fail because you've added too much

– painting can also be a process of taking away. For a long time – and I still do this occasionally – I made paintings by putting on the paint and taking it off, leaving a little bit. I was trying to get away from literally descriptive things, towards a barer, emptier space.

Now, I'm putting things back in. The still life of flowers ['Carte d'Embarquement (Flowers)'] was the first painting I made for the show. I was listening to a lot of Philip Glass, his piano études. He was once quoted [in Tim Page's 1993 article 'Music in 12 Parts'] as saying that having 'taken everything out with my early works ... it was now time to decide just what I wanted to put back in'. That's just what I wanted. I felt like I was really struggling with that. Wanting to use paint, but having such a hard time getting away from the literalness of it sometimes.

Q. THE WHITE REVIEW —— Your paintings have a particular aesthetic, which is this very fluid, watery brushstroke. It's quite unique – no other artist's work looks like this. Can you just talk us through the process?
A. ELIZABETH PEYTON —— When I was younger I painted on found glass. I really loved the fast surface, as paint doesn't absorb into glass. Now I use a wood panel that I put layer after layer of gesso on, sanding in between until it's like glass... which similarly to the glass lets me have the kind of movement I want in my work.

In a sense, making the support is the first part of the painting. Sometimes I'm thinking forward: I see lines building up when I'm using the taping knife, because naturally it's not the most perfect surface. They can guide the composition.

Q. THE WHITE REVIEW —— Do you sketch things out first, or work directly onto the surface of the painting?

A. ELIZABETH PEYTON —— The thing is the thing.

Q. THE WHITE REVIEW —— So sketching and painting are one and the same?

A. ELIZABETH PEYTON —— Yes, which relates back to movement. That record of figuring it out is an exciting part of the painting. It's also so challenging, to figure it out from nothing.

Q. THE WHITE REVIEW —— Your portraits tend to be of people that you know, as well as some people that you don't know but that you are drawn to in some way. Is there a big difference in painting someone from the life, to use the antiquated phrase, as opposed to painting from a photograph? Because you do both.

A. ELIZABETH PEYTON —— I'll often use both for a single portrait. I'll work from life and then work from photos, and then maybe from memory or even other photos. Life tends to get a little literal. I like the magical things that come from my own bad photography, or from photos found on the internet. They might contain something that you would never see in real life.

Q. THE WHITE REVIEW —— Something a bit off.

A. ELIZABETH PEYTON —— Yes, like a blurring or a heightening of colour, some degeneration. I get really excited about things like that.

Q. THE WHITE REVIEW —— So the paintings are almost palimpsest, a layering of the drawing or painting from life with photography. Is it strange painting yourself, as in 'Dirty Pink Heron' (2016)? Because sitting for a portrait – and I think you were the first artist I ever sat for – can be a very exposing experience.

A. ELIZABETH PEYTON —— It's very exposing for me too. By asking someone to sit for me I'm saying that I really want to be with you, spend some time with you, get to know you, look at you. It's a very particular kind of attention. It makes me feel vulnerable, but it's so tender. I often think that people don't really know what other people look like. People generalise even the people they know so well. The shorthand of the person with the tie, and the coloured hair, and stuff. But they don't really see. The person can look so different.

Q. THE WHITE REVIEW —— Genre is and always has been important to your work. As far as I know you're not somebody who's painted abstract works; you've always painted portraits or still lifes. You've worked within classical genres, but you have fun with them. There's a dialogue between them, so a portrait could be a still life, or a still life could be a portrait.

A. ELIZABETH PEYTON —— I don't really think about genre. I mean, I never thought about portraiture much. The work just has to function as a picture.

Q. THE WHITE REVIEW —— Other passions find their way into your work. Music influences your work in multiple ways, most obviously in your choice of musicians as sitters, whether classical, punk, rock and roll, or rap. But is there an element of synaesthesia, because you listen to music when you paint, right?

A. ELIZABETH PEYTON —— I don't have synaesthesia exactly. I do have this voice thing, when a portrait I'm doing is getting close to really feeling like the person, I can hear their voice. Like I can hear you talking, it just happens.

Q. THE WHITE REVIEW —— When I sat for you, it a particular world. There's the relationship between the sitter and artist, but also the fact of being in your studio and your house. It's very domestic. It's not a warehouse studio that's separate from where you live. Your dog is there, you choose the music.

A· ELIZABETH PEYTON —— Whether consciously or not, I am aware that everything I bring into my home could potentially be part of the picture.

Q· THE WHITE REVIEW —— In terms of being drawn to things or images, your recent work includes versions of existing paintings. 'Two Women (after Courbet)' (2015), for example, relates to Courbet's 'Le Sommeil' (1866); and 'Knights Dreaming (K) after EBJ' (2016) to Edward Burne-Jones's 'The Rose Bower' (1890).

A· ELIZABETH PEYTON —— I recently went to see the series [of which 'The Rose Bower' is a part] by Burne-Jones, which was based on Tennyson's 'The Sleeping Beauty'. My paint-ing is after the first picture in the series ['The Briar Wood']. I'd only seen them on the inter-net before that.

Q· THE WHITE REVIEW —— How do you find these things? How do you know when they will become part of your work?

A· ELIZABETH PEYTON —— I want to get close to it, I want to know how it works. In this case, too, I'd been thinking a lot about knights, and Tristan from Wagner's TRISTAN UND ISOLDE. This came together with something in my mind, something I really wanted to see. I was thinking about bands and the way young men are together. The way they love each other – that is very much a part of this painting. I've never let that out of my mouth before. But it's something I thought about quite a lot.

Q· THE WHITE REVIEW —— If you ignore the clothing, they could be musicians on tour...

A· ELIZABETH PEYTON —— Yes. They're tired. They trust each other. They're in the middle of nowhere. But they have each other.

Q· THE WHITE REVIEW —— Your work has really oscillated between very contemporary people and images – New York in the 1990s, or certain musicians, people and places who are very much of the now – and things from the past. Yet they're all treated equally. Were you always a painter of historical things?

A· ELIZABETH PEYTON —— Yes, at the beginning more so. Proust was a revelation to me when I was young, his understanding at the end of À LA RECHERCHE..., that it's all present, every-thing is continual.

Q· THE WHITE REVIEW —— And that's a key thing in your work. If we narrow it down to music, your work encompasses the more edgy, raw, punk end of things, in a very real way, but there's also a yearning for something more innocent.

A· ELIZABETH PEYTON —— Yes, but one could say Wagner's quite edgy. Not to be defensive about classical music, but it's painful and it's raw.

Q· THE WHITE REVIEW —— So is it just that in people and images and music, you have a singular taste, irrespective of from where or when it comes?

A· ELIZABETH PEYTON —— Yes, but I'm not the first to say that. Baudelaire said that the ideal artist is timeless. Like the Titian painting in the Frick, 'Portrait of a Man in a Red Cap', or Giorgione's 'Portrait of a Young Man' in the Staatliche... I've made copies of both those paintings, actually. These things contain the humanity of the relationship between two people in a room. If you get to the right place in art, it's all alive – or it's alive forever.

Q· THE WHITE REVIEW —— You've painted some of your subjects – Jonathan Horowitz, Nick Relph – over a long period. Is it interesting to paint the passage of time?

A. ELIZABETH PEYTON —— Yes, it's so interesting But it's not just the physical changes. Recently I was re-photographing stills from Luchino Visconti's LUDWIG (1972). I made a lot of pictures from that film [about King Ludwig II, Wagner's patron] when I was 20 or 21. At that age I didn't want to know anything about Wagner at all, but now I want to know everything about Wagner. So I'm appreciating LUDWIG in a different way.

Q. THE WHITE REVIEW —— Is film important to you? Are there directors you look to?

A. ELIZABETH PEYTON —— Visconti, clearly. I think I'm attracted to filmmakers like François Truffaut who can make an anecdotal narrative film that somehow filters its time through its subject.

Q. THE WHITE REVIEW —— It distils or channels everything.

A. ELIZABETH PEYTON —— Yes, like in THE REVENANT. It's so poetic and beautiful, but also powerfully political.

Q. THE WHITE REVIEW —— Part of your work is about looking and desire and beauty. The idea of the female gaze and feminist art criticism of the 1970s – was that something you ever actively engaged in?

A. ELIZABETH PEYTON —— It's always been very natural rather than theoretical, though of course I am aware of that history. I think that if I was a man my pictures would be more highly regarded as portraits, and I would be questioned less about my 'obsessiveness'. It is considered normal that a man should paint talented and successful people to whom he is attracted! There's a higher ideal in that. My work is pretty 'feminine' in the sense that it's emotional, it's feeling.

Q. THE WHITE REVIEW —— I don't want to go back to failure, but I love thinking about it. What percentage of the images don't work?

A. ELIZABETH PEYTON —— It used to be much higher, because I would paint a lot more. But the failure rate is still significant.

Q. THE WHITE REVIEW —— Your press release for the latest show cites TRISTAN UND ISOLDE, which we've talked about. Is literature an influence upon your work?

A. ELIZABETH PEYTON —— Yes, that was maybe the first thing. When I was younger, I would make pictures based on what I was reading, pictures of things that didn't exist. I still feel that way about the pictures I make. Something that doesn't exist and is missing and so I want to make it.

Q. THE WHITE REVIEW —— Do you consider yourself as part of a particular lineage, as an artist?

A. ELIZABETH PEYTON —— Yes absolutely. Yesterday I saw the Eugène Delacroix show [at the National Gallery] and I thought... I mean, I don't want to elevate myself to that. But I feel very comfortable with the way he went about painting. I feel in the family of, or I want to be in the family of, Delacroix, van Dyck, Manet, Sargent, Gustave Moreau. I am very grateful that I can do this, but also feel like it's a responsibility. There's the duty to reflect on what's in my time, be it old or new.

NICHOLAS CULLINAN, FEBRUARY 2016

EXPERIENCE
IN GROUPS

BY

GEOFFREY G. O'BRIEN

EXPERIENCE IN GROUPS

I have a hunch my experience is
All the plastic of those years
Earlier and later were
Young as a company, living
Especially by day or night
Through an illness of believing
In something still to come, to be done
By all or none, not any

You could state the case for
Becoming more than one of.
The problem with pronouns is you
Says more and less than wanted,
Frequently all the time. Thus is living
Made to resemble its cure.
This has been proved and reproved,
Proven even. It is an hour

Then another one. Laugh if you like
Taking from the others around you
A faintly running pleasure in
The cancellation of such hopes as are
Possible to have, ones that thrived
Then throve, still do, don't, are
A crowded power, or the power
To think so, where thinking is

Responding to silent commands,
Advice released from compartments
To join the crowd ahead, speak out
Or up and from the fouled forms,
The manufactured weather sliding
Into place, almost distinct from time.
This is the hour of jolie–laide.
No, this is, and I am going

To wait for another where
Although and because are not
Secretly allied or open
Synonyms united in
Their influence. This making of
Names into cries has got to stop,
This reliance on facial recognition,
On the intimacy of apathy,

Of hours that need to slow
Then stop, become space, begin
Reading at a rally, get thrown out,
Check themselves, record the whole
Experience, post it, cross–
Post it, like it themselves, delete it,
Take it back, apologise,
Suspend the account, then and only

Then start a new one, barely use it,
Has got to stop if we are going
To be at least all, lucid, ludic,
In and out of the game, definite
Article, the genuine, sheltering
In a movement between to and from
As though we were allowed,
As though the hypothetical were

Real as your neighborhood bar,
As a recipe on the internet,
As passion out mistaking itself
For a jade helm, for exercise,
A kind of holy and continuous
Publication of the instantaneous
Ruling everything around me,
The new life its death has, has

Got to stop without becoming
A monument, a gap driven through
The end of the headland, burnt church
Of space solemnised back into blue
Blue water, security theatre
Of its waves, that just keep coming
To our shores in a pattern without
Intention, that have so fascinated

Poets and children, waves that look
Like they've been kicked out
Of the republic of elsewhere,
Are from but not yet to, upon
Which we can confer some interim
Papers, refuse their faces, turn away,
Turn them back to unseen, evidence
We've been watching for a long time

Come to light, chatter and pledge
Finally reaching the shores of the first
Person plural, worn smooth,
Translucent, picked up and discounted.
Hard to know what to guard against
When the whole ocean is preparation,
When there is nothing of value to protect
On all matter of earths

The official one conceals. That's my hunch,
Some towers, the cable underground,
The moment or monument everything is
At risk of becoming, the bottom line
That can be drawn between any two points
In the sand. I have my go-bag,
Pronouns for each eventuality
Or the likelihood of one, one already

Scripted if undecided whether
It totally will have hasn't happened
Yet. There are no reports other than
The sound of three days in a row
Of rain; the dog senses nothing;
The dawn winds its usual withdrawal
Through pinks; anchors' mouths
Don't have it to say, that hour

Still to come the water closes
Easily over, the plane can't catch,
Yet I check for by drawing breath,
Talking to the corporate person
Of the morning when it appears to my left
As woman and dog, the news
Before the news hits so softly
There is nothing behind it.

Especially at any time of day
I find I'm confusing various waves
Of the present with those still about to,
Discovering what I'm doing as
I'll do it, unsafe as always, at all
Speeds, a kind of retrospective
Procrastination to keep from thinking
How bad completely fine feels

With we not yet on the table,
Under it where the dog begs,
Money changes hands, assumes
Its temporary forms of altered mood,
Music you can see. The hour is
Not around you but between us
On its knees, pushed down, laid out,
Triptych of the tenses each

Tense acting alone is
Independently in concert.
That three that has pursued me through
Us into you at the level of the cell,
The cloud, units difficult
To quantify, keep track of even
If sensed in their sometime assemblies.
And the timetable also vague,

It could be next year or in two
Or whatever the number after that
Will be by the time we're beached there
Where fire and water are synonyms,
Synonym the polite term for ally,
Ally a way of pretending solidarity
Across difference which is itself
Globally pretended. All this

You must fly through, over
And over like a wave that doesn't break
Because it can reform, replacing
All its clear blue constitutive parts
Until they are allied with time.
My hunch is time has been
Tasked with making the world seem
Renewable, so each change

Is a stranger, part threat, part friend
Of a friend of a friend you can combine
In different ratios, producing new
Kinships among the available
Doomed but persistent norms.
I'm still talking about events as children
Or militia because they are equally
At home sheltering in a place

For the genuine, a protocol for dealing
With dangerous or recalcitrant
Material. If you want to understand
The history of speech, its relationship
To crowds and night, the implied push
Of heaving water to the left or right,
Imagine losing your friend in a riot
Or parade, at the speed of assembly,

In an era without technologies
For communicating other than voice,
Paper, and horn, no plan in place
For reuniting your parts, followed by
Long days of attempting to find her in all
The locals, the rainy squares, then think
Of how those limits on speech
And rapid togetherness had conditioned you

Even prior to the loss of your person,
How what you were unable to do
Determined how and what you did,
How you met and parted, even down
To your posture and the rolling nature
Of your gait, then try to think of what
We can't do now and how it affects
What we try anyway to accomplish

Then subtract the first person plural
And you are speaking inside the wave
Passing through the divided headland
Looking onto the island of the present
Where it happened. Then already
Calling your family to try to explain this
Using the language of negotiation
With those with whom you won't,

Describing the island's "memory wound"
And the "voided void" of the tower with no
Exit or entrance which however manages
To weep visitors every hour;
You can hear your own breathing
Better in the dark, where to stand
Still feels like flying underground.
And now your work, which is ours,

Can truly begin. You will need
At least two others and a negative
Capacity for sustaining unfinished
Attention to the breaks in the clouds;
Song will be of no use to you
And thus may be frequently employed,
Splintering the total night into
Unpredictable sets of smaller parts;

Mask up the lower part of the face
Or paint it in that new way
That briefly frustrates detection; sing through it
To your child whether you have one
Or no, or not yet, have lost him
In the crowd of years; make sure
There is ground beneath you, or water
Or air, their various conspiracies.

Get up, then go back when she calls,
When there's outcry or instant
Messaging or what Utoya sounds like
It means in English, or Paris, Berlin,
The long war journal of cities
And villages, Mandi Khel, Ghar Laley
In Waziristan, and the body of all
Who have lived in conditions, night,

Day, both coming closer until
They sort of meet twice then wander away
Like recurring monuments tend to;
Mention those, their embarrassment,
The logistics of container ships,
Border checks and dreaming one's way
Back through speech to families of origin,
That stockpile of experience assembled

Over many years so you
Were ready to act when the time came,
Though it hadn't, hasn't and won't,
You have to go out and meet it
Squarely by deciding it has
Ripened to a habitable absence, like a home
In an era, where one could sleep
Or you do, while the futures divide.

LISTENING
TO YOURSELF

BY

LAWRENCE ABU HAMDAN

IN THE EARLY 2000s, Belgium, Germany, Holland, Sweden, Switzerland, the United Kingdom, New Zealand and Australia began implementing a screening technique for asylum seekers and undocumented migrants called 'Language Analysis for the Determination of Origin' (LADO). This attempts to determine if the accent of an undocumented migrant corroborates their claim of national identity. For example, the authorities aim to determine – based on accent alone – whether a Somali is from Mogadishu (a legitimate place from which to claim asylum) or in fact from northern Somalia (considered a safe place to live and thus to be deported back to). The tender to carry out these tests was mostly won by two private Swedish companies, Sprakab and Verified. These companies conducted phone interviews with asylum applicants in the target countries, using Sweden's largely unemployed former refugee population as a resource of informants to listen in on calls and conduct interviews. These informants' non-scientific assertions on where they thought people 'really' came from were then reworked by linguists, who bolstered the claims with international phonetic symbols and turned them into forensic reports for use in court in the target countries.

When academic linguists throughout the world were alerted to this flawed screening process, they began to contest its ideology of monolingualism. Linguists insisted that the voice is not a bureaucratic document, but rather a biography, and an index of everyone you have ever spoken to. The itinerant lives of refugees meant that their voices in particular should not be used as a national identifier. They argued that while the informants conducting the interviews may speak the same language as the applicant, they frequently were not from the same place. This could affect the dialogue and the quality of the data. After hundreds of wrongful deportations, governments finally began to listen to these campaigning linguists. Yet rather than scrap LADO, they insidiously incorporated the critiques, deciding that since dialogue was rendering the tests unscientific, they would use monologues instead. Now, rather than soliciting speech in an interview, asylum seekers were expected to simply speak for fifteen minutes non-stop. They were free to say anything they wanted, because nothing they said had any relevance. Only their accents mattered. One of these accounts is reproduced over the following pages: the words this time emptied of their voice. What seems at first like an anxious stream of consciousness is in fact a precise account of the weaponisation of freedom of speech, which is reaching its nightmare conclusion in today's liberal democracies.

———————

AUDITOR: Off you go.

ASYLUM SPEAKER: Umm... Good morning. I am a married woman. I have two children, [breathes in] that is I have two daughters, very pretty [breathes in]. One of them is 15 years old, the eldest, [breathes in] and the youngest is still 12 years old. My daughters I feel are the most precious thing in my life. [Sharp intake of breath] Umm... I feel that happiness and the whole world come from them. [Breathes in] How much I love them I cannot possibly describe to anyone at all, because they are the soul and spirit inside of me and my body. I wish for God Almighty to keep them for me and that I be destined to be able to raise them as best I can so they are productive in society. [Breathes in] I would like to talk a little, I am remembering now, and often remember, my school. How I used to go to school when I was little, how they used to treat us in school. [Breathes in] Maybe there are some very nice things that one can remember, but there are also some very painful things. I studied and learned and was very good at school, I always liked going to school. Even if I was sick, nothing mattered [breathes in], whatever it was. I used to always go to school, even if I was tired and sick. Although I went through some very difficult experiences [large sigh], I experienced some difficult health issues, I was very distressed as I had to undergo surgeries [breathes in], but in spite of that, to me school was always the core of my life. [Breathes in] And I was very studious, I never missed a class. Umm... one time, and I can never forget this... One time I was at school and I was in tenth grade, [breathes in] I was a little late one morning. In order to make it on time and not be very late, I started running. I ran and ran [stretches word] from my parents' home until I reached school. I went in, our first class was Arabic language [breathes in]. I entered, I got there and I entered, I knocked on the door and I entered. Our teacher was there, and she had started giving the class. So she looked at my face and said [imitates a stern tone], 'What's up with you? Where were you?' I told her [imitates an innocent tone], 'I am very sorry teacher, I apologise, but I am late because the alarm didn't ring at home.' She looked at me and started berating me, using nasty words, I can't repeat them because when I remember them and repeat them, I feel a lot of pain and a lot of pressure that I don't need in my life. [Breathes in] Anyway the important part of the story is that she said, 'So you are late to school and you have make-up on?' I told her, 'I am not wearing make-up teacher,' because my mum and dad were very strict about this, [raises the pitch of her voice] 'It's shameful for a girl to wear make-up, a girl should not dress this way, a girl should not speak this way.' [Breathes in] So all the time, thank God, they had raised us in the best way. I swore to her by the Qur'an that I hadn't done anything, that I wasn't wearing make-up on my face, that I had never used any [breathes in]. She opened her bag and took out a Kleenex tissue, and the colour of the tissue, I remember, was white. [Breathes in] And she started rubbing and rubbing [stretches word] and

E

rubbing my face, and my face was getting redder and redder. She'd rub and look at the tissue and see that it was clean, there was nothing on it, nothing that indicated that I had make-up on my face. But because my skin is white, and I'd been running, and I felt very hot from running, my face and cheeks turned very red [*breathes in*]. She looked at me and said, 'Go [*short pause*], get out of my face and sit in your place' [*breathes in*]. Although I was one of the best students in her class, [*swallows*] but what she thought at the time, I have no idea [*breathes in*]. Unfortunately some memories are painful [*discreetly clears throat, swallows*], but nevertheless, some experiences that a person goes through are very difficult to forget [*fingers tapping on table*]. [*Breathes in*] Another thing, also one time at school [*exhales*], umm… the teacher responsible for discipline at school. I came to school, and my mother had forgotten to wash my trousers the day before, my school trousers, the uniform that we all wore. So I had to wear other trousers. And I went to school. The teacher saw me, or the supervisor. She said to me, 'Come here you why aren't you wearing the complete uniform?' [*Fingers tapping on table resumes*] I told her my mother didn't have time to wash it, what could I do I had to wear whatever trousers I had…

TYPIST: [*Whispers something inaudible to the auditor*]

ASYLUM SPEAKER: [*Breathes in, catches breath*], or different colour trousers [*resumes breathing in*]. In order to punish me, she made me take off my shoes…

TYPIST: [*Whispers to the auditor, louder this time but still hard to make out*]

ASYLUM SPEAKER: …and stand in a pool of water, and the water was very very cold, it was ice cold, I remember that very well, because I was in the ninth grade then [*breathes in*]. It was very cold, and she made me take off my shoes, as well as my socks, everything, and to stand in the pool. When I got very cold and I felt that I could no longer stand there with my feet in the cold water, I started shouting and crying. When I shouted and cried, she took me out of the pool. Then, and as a result of this, I had renal colic because I was suffering from a kidney stone. If I caught the cold, I would have an episode, the pain wouldn't stop until I was admitted to the hospital and given tranquiliser and painkiller shots [*sighs*]. Of course the director came out because of the sound and noise we made in the schoolyard. She said, 'What's wrong with you?' [*Voice hardens*] I told her, 'I have a pain in my kidney, [*raises pitch of voice*] I can't take the pain anymore, I need medicine. Call my dad so he can come and take me to the hospital.' Of course the school director knew my father well and had a very good relationship with him. And she used to visit us at home sometimes. [*Breathes in*] When she saw me like this she told her, 'Couldn't you find another student than this one to

E

punish?' She spoke to the teacher, 'She's one of the very polite students in school this one, [*breathes in*] she doesn't neglect her duties, she's well raised by her parents, why did you do this to her today?' The supervisor told her [*imitates a belligerent tone*], 'Because she has changed her trousers, she's wearing different trousers.' She thought of course that I had liked to embellish and beautify myself and that sort of thing, but I didn't have that intention or thought at all. It was just that I didn't find other trousers to wear because the other ones were dirty [*discreetly clears throat, breathes in*]. Anyhow she took me to the administration, to the administration room [*breathes in*], the director, she sat me down there for a bit, she brought me a hot cup of tea, and gave me a pill, a painkiller from her drawer. And she called my dad. Of course my dad came and took me from there in the car to the hospital. As a result, I spent the night at the hospital, and they had to do a surgical operation. [*Foot tapping on floor*] Now I'd like to speak a little about my childhood memories. [*In the background, the sound of a key turning in a lock*] I was living happily, I remember, with my parents, my sisters and brothers. [*Breathes in*] We are, praise God, a large family, may the evil eye be shamed. I had many girlfriends at school, and also in the area I was living in [*swallows*], but the dearest one to my heart and best friend, she's my lifelong friend, her name was Serene. May God ease her way and give her happiness wherever she goes. She was someone a person could really trust [*breathes in*], a person who deserves all my appreciation and respect. [*Breathes in*] Because she is someone who stood by me through many difficulties and through life's trials, that one naturally goes through. Of course life is full of them, and every person has certainly gone through a lot, and yet, this person I would always feel standing by me. I remember, even in 1980, when I had my operation, how she stood by me, how she cried [*pronounces word emphatically*], when they took me to the operating room, how when I came out and woke up from the anesthesia, I felt her standing beside me, waiting for me to open my eyes. She felt with my pain, and laughed with my laughter. She used to be with me the whole time, we went to the same school, the same class, even the same bus [*catches breath*] where we sat together. A wonderful person, I can't describe her. But I also had another friend, we used to be together all the time the three of us, our parents used to call us 'the merry trio'. [*Breathes in*] We used to hang out together, we slept over at each other's house sometimes. Once, she and I, on New Year's Eve, I told my parents that I would like to spend it at her house [*breathes in*], to hang out just the two of us. Her parents weren't home, they were going out somewhere [*breathes in*]. We sat together, she had prepared food, she had made *mulukhiyyeh* and other delicious dishes that we liked, we stayed up late just the two of us, there was nobody else there at all at all [*swallows*]. We stayed up almost until the next morning [*breathes in*], we didn't sleep until maybe after six o'clock in the morning [*breathes in*]. [*Chair leg scrapes on the linoleum floor*] We would talk about how our school day went, what our childhood was like, we talked about our

E

shared memories, the bitter and the sweet, and sometimes laughed at each other. Anyhow, we spent the whole night drinking juice and drinking tea, and smoking also of course, smoking was forbidden, it was shameful for a girl to smoke, but maybe to me it was something new, and I felt like trying it. But now that I'm grown up, I feel that my parents were right, they used to always tell me, [*imitating strict tone*] 'Don't smoke, it's shameful.' Maybe they said it was shameful for a girl to smoke, but at the same time, they shouldn't have just said it is shameful, they should have explained to me why it was shameful, maybe they could have said that it is dangerous for the health, maybe I could have been more convinced, but just that it's shameful, that I shouldn't do it because it's shameful, why not tell me from the beginning that it is dangerous, healthwise, that it hurts the lungs, that it harms a person's health, even fitness decreases with time because of it, with the years and with age, you can no longer breathe normally, it causes constriction in the arteries, it could lead to heart attacks God forbid, it could cause many health problems. [*Breathes in sharply*] But unfortunately this health education was not at all available to any of our parents. Maybe, when they forbade us to do certain things, they thought, first and foremost, that it was shameful, because society said it was shameful, because it is shameful for a girl to go out, it is shameful for a girl to come in, it is shameful for a girl to smoke, it is shameful for a girl for example, to do this or that. At least explain to us, you're supposed to raise some kind of awareness in us, [*breathes in*] something that I used to read about a lot in books, and it was a hobby of mine, reading, I liked books. [*Breathes in*] I read many books. Until now, the story that I can never forget as long as I live [*breathes in*] is THE MOTHER, by Maxim Gorky. I liked his novels a lot. I also read, with my friend that I am speaking about, Serene, I read a lot of books by al–Manfaluti. Until now I remember one of the stories, it was called 'Majdaline', it was very beautiful. Praise God books were always accessible to me [*breathes in*], I loved reading, I liked, what I liked most of all was to sit on the couch and just read. [*Breathes in*] I wasn't that much into watching television, because I always felt like: so what are all these programmes? [*Breathes in*] They are just entertainment, but not useful mentally, there's no culture in them, no educational value, whether in terms of health awareness or any other kind [*breathes in*]. So I wasn't too interested in sitting and watching TV series, very rarely, although I felt that the rest of the family was. And maybe that's the time that we as a family would sit together, we'd sit, eat together, and watch television together [*breathes in*]. Especially during the evenings of Ramadan, may God allow it many returns, always in prosperity and good health for all. It was a month that brought together the family. Our customs during Ramadan were very enjoyable, we used to prepare a variety of dishes, [*swallows*] my mum used to always cook *sayyadiyyeh*, which the whole family [*breathes in*] loves. We'd sit, gather together and eat, she used to like making tabbouleh, and we liked it a lot, especially when we were little, and I still love it and prepare it for my children, and

E

my girls like it very very much. They always tell me, 'Mum cook for us, make us *umlukhiyych*, makc us tabbouleh, make us fattoush', the dishes that they like and enjoy very much. I try as much as I can to make the food that they like, always. [*Breathes in*] Anyway the nights of Ramadan were the most beautiful nights of the year, especially on the night of Eid when the Takbir for the feast would begin, it was a very very beautiful thing. We would sit and make the *kaak* biscuits together, the *kaak* for Eid, we'd get together with the neighbours [*breathes in*]. These were the beautiful moments and occasions. [*Sharp intake of breath*]

AUDITOR: OK, thank you, that is enough.

TRANSLATION BY MASHA REFKA

E

INTERVIEW

WITH

GARY INDIANA

IN JULY 2015, *T: THE NEW YORK TIMES STYLE MAGAZINE* gathered twenty-eight 'artists, writers, performers, musicians and intellectuals who defined New York's inimitable and electrifying cultural scene of the late 1970s and early '80s', for a photo shoot entitled 'They Made New York'. Among them were Philip Glass, Chuck Close, Susan Sarandon, Fran Lebowitz and DJ Kool Herc. Almost everyone smiles, except for one man in the middle, who carries the face not of a celebrant but of a survivor. This man is the writer, artist and filmmaker Gary Indiana.

Born Gary Hoisington, Indiana was raised in Derry, New Hampshire. At 16 he was accepted to the University of California, Berkeley, only to drop out shortly after. He would crash around various communes until he found his place among a group of filmmakers developing what became known as 'narrative porn' – smut with a storyline, which would come to resemble modern reality TV. In 1973, Indiana arrived in Los Angeles, where he was hired as a receptionist for an inner-city medical clinic and had access to 'an endless supply of pharmaceutical amphetamines'. He took occupancy at the Bryson Apartment Hotel, a complex once considered 'the finest apartment-house west of New York City', and later made noir-famous by Raymond Chandler, who used it as a backdrop in his 1943 story 'The Lady in the Lake'. By 1977 the Bryson was inhabited by junkies and dregs; Indiana, too, was falling apart. A near death experience sent him packing to Manhattan, a place that to him had already had its moment: 'I didn't come to New York,' he points out, 'until 1978.'

Defining Indiana by location, occupation or time is a tricky endeavour. In the early eighties, he acted in experimental films, put on plays and wrote art criticism for *THE VILLAGE VOICE*, before publishing his debut story collection *SCAR TISSUE AND OTHER STORIES* in 1987. His first novel, *HORSE CRAZY* (1989), in which an older male writer falls for a younger former junkieturned-waiter, is set against the backdrop of an AIDS-ravaged New York. The writer character closely resembles Indiana, distilling his life into literature in a fashion that predates the work of Ben Lerner or Sheila Heti. This interest in documentation – of self or otherwise – characterises Indiana's prose: for Indiana, merely living is a poetic statement.

Over the past decade Indiana has frequently decamped from New York to Havana, a place that features prominently in his first memoir, *I CAN GIVE YOU ANYTHING BUT LOVE*. So too does his time in Los Angeles, which he recollects with his trademark sardonicism. New York is notably absent, as are the many projects that would accredit him for the *NEW YORK TIMES* shoot. When I pressed him about their omission, he gave me a wry smile: 'Why do you care?'

This interview took place last November in Café Lucien, in New York's East Village. Beforehand, I'd Googled his image and found a man with short dyed blond hair dotted with leopard spots and wrapped in a black fur coat. In a sunlit corner, I found a much less intimidating figure sitting at the table nearest the sun-drenched windows. I introduced myself just as he bit into a slice of table bread. Rather than starting things off on the wrong foot, Gary took a moment to chew, sipped his water and smiled. He said, in a voice both friendly and slightly curled, 'I'm ready to meet you now.'

---

^{Q.} THE WHITE REVIEW — *I CAN GIVE YOU ANYTHING BUT LOVE* is divided between Cuba and earlier memories of growing up, and most of it focused on your time in Los Angeles. Why these two periods?

^{A.} GARY INDIANA — The first drafts of the book were longer than the finished thing, and contained more episodes in Europe and New York. I made a gradual decision to take out almost anything dealing with well-known individuals, and with myself becoming a 'public person'. I didn't want to write the kind of book people buy for gossip value. So I removed almost everything except my early life in California, among people who weren't famous, and later times in Cuba – again, among people nobody's ever heard of.

I didn't know what I was writing or why I was writing it until I'd worked on it for a couple of years; it was a fumbling process of clarifying certain questions I'd always had in my brain, and maybe answering a few, first of all. I didn't expect to write so much about my friendship with Ferd Eggan [an influential AIDS awareness activist, he later served as Los Angeles' AIDS coordinator from 1993 to 2001]. It was an important friendship in some ways, and in other ways it had almost nothing to do with my everyday existence, or with his, for that matter, even when we were both living in the same city – but the nervous, intermittent bond between us suggested a way of organising the book, to some extent. Writing about it freed me from certain myths I'd spun around that friendship for years. For instance, that Ferd always felt that he should've been doing what I was doing in life, and that I kind of felt that I should have been doing what he was doing. That may have been slightly true, inconsistently true. He was, in fact, sometimes a frustrated artist and writer, and a little part of me sometimes felt guilty for not becoming a political activist. But over the years I had exaggerated this in my mind into something of huge symbolic importance, and it really wasn't such a striking theme in our relationship.

^{Q.} THE WHITE REVIEW — When writing these relationships, is it possible to depict them without making people unhappy?

^{A.} GARY INDIANA — Probably not, unless you ignore everything you know about them. If they happen to be dead, however you depict them is going to make somebody who knew them unhappy. Ferd is someone I knew, so to speak, from a particular angle, often at variance from the roles he played in his professional life, and his other friendships; all I mean by that is that we are all different people with different people. As Witold Gombrowicz said, people create one another in an inter-human collaboration that's never exactly the same from one interaction to the next. I can't imagine that Ferd's other friends would find my portrait of him at all adequate. They knew a slightly different person than I did. Moreover, they probably knew him much better than I did.

^{Q.} THE WHITE REVIEW — There's practically no mention of yourself as a writer or an artist in the book. People often read memoirs with a vested interest in someone's life, but you only open a few windows, rather than unlock the house.

^{A.} GARY INDIANA — I think it's pretty clear from the book that I had a hard time doing anything. I didn't even believe I could do anything until, quite honestly, I was almost 30. I don't think my artistic process, or my career as a writer or artist, would be interesting for anybody to read about, unless you talk about collaborations with other people. But the abjection and cluelessness of my early life

– that's compelling, because so many people experience the same sort of thing at that age. And Cuba, too, because until very recently, it was still an exotic place.

I realised after working on the memoir for a long time that I wanted to avoid recounting events that could be construed as the 'true' versions of stories I'd already recounted in fictional form, since what one does in writing fiction is so widely and often quite maliciously misconstrued. So that was one consideration, avoiding material I'd used in fiction in one way or another. At the same time, I discovered that writing a memoir, if you're actually a writer, involves formal and aesthetic choices that make it impossible to tell 'the whole truth and nothing but the truth', as if you were giving sworn testimony in court. Court transcripts make pretty dull reading.

I actually hate contemporary memoirs. Almost without exception, I hate the whole genre. The whole memoir genre, the comparable reality TV craze – all of it is corrupt and pathological. The more people claim what they're telling or showing is real, the further it is from the truth. People never tell the whole truth about themselves, and only ever tell part of the truth from behind the safety of a mask. Why do you think fiction was invented in the first place? A good novel is a thousand times more revealing than a memoir. Maybe Rousseau or Chateaubriand or Saint Augustine can be considered exceptions, but I doubt even that.

Q THE WHITE REVIEW — Could the omission of your New York years also have been a response to the fetishisation of that era? There is far more literature about New York in that era than about 1970s Los Angeles. What was Los Angeles like at that time?

A GARY INDIANA — All the recent necrophiliac nostalgia for the late 1970s and early 1980s New York – a period that I did draw on a lot in HORSE CRAZY and RENT BOY, also in DO EVERYTHING IN THE DARK – is so off-base that I didn't want to engage with it at all. After I came to New York in 1978, I experienced about three years of chaotic, impoverished, youthful excitement and desperate creative improvisation, followed by a decade of non-stop death of people around me from AIDS, while scrambling for survival the whole time by writing journalism. New York was never the same after the epidemic. In fact, it's been a horribly depressing, punitive city to live in ever since, thanks to the disappearance of so many vital people, and thanks to real estate developers and Wall Street. But people who keep dredging up what a great place New York was thirty or forty years ago should just shut up and open a funeral home, where nobody minds if you talk about dead people all day.

If you want an idea of what LA was like in the seventies, you should watch THE KILLING OF A CHINESE BOOKIE by John Cassavetes, whom I knew back then. You can see the way the merciless sunlight hit the Sunset Strip at noon, how the freeways were practically deserted after 10 p.m. – it really was a different place, a haunted backwater. Nothing was happening except punk, which emerged in '74 or '75. But LA is 760 square miles, and punk happened in what amounted to two or three blocks of that space. Otherwise, it was a dead town. It was a pleasant place to feel dead, too. I love LA. Even today, you can find a stillness there that you can't in New York, despite the architectural infill, which is really astonishing. You can still arrive at the dead zone. That's not always such a bad feeling, when everything just stops. You can also have a social life that isn't mired in nostalgia or hobbled by a completely hateful and physically ugly environment. There's a very different feeling at 2 a.m. in LA than in New York. A feeling that life is still possible.

Q· THE WHITE REVIEW —— You mention in the book that your apartment in the Bryson building was featured in the 1990 film *THE GRIFTERS* and then later in *MAGNOLIA*, the 1999 film directed by Paul Thomas Anderson. Was that a coincidence?

A· GARY INDIANA —— I've always thought that whoever wrote *THE GRIFTERS*, or Stephen Frears, who directed it, must've lived at the Bryson when I did, because it was very much like it is in the movie – an apartment hotel, with a front desk and so forth, managed by the same type of gossipy old Midwestern windbag. But I didn't know Stephen Frears, or P. T. Anderson. Anyway, it's not my apartment in *THE GRIFTERS* – though what had been my apartment windows are featured in *MAGNOLIA*. Complete coincidence in both cases.

LA is full of those types of coincidence. For the most part, no one bats an eye. I recently acted in a Laura Parnes film called *TOUR WITHOUT END*. I played a version of Dave Mustaine, the guitarist who got kicked out of Metallica. One night we were filming in this club in Brooklyn. A woman was performing, afterwards we got into a conversation, and it turned out that her parents owned Circus of Books, the porn bookstore that was adjacent to my first LA apartment on North La Jolla Avenue in the early '70s. They were apparently fairly conventional, middle-class Jewish business people; her mother would say things like, 'Oh I've got a carton of crack pipes coming in this week.' Business as usual.

Q· THE WHITE REVIEW —— You're going back to LA in a few days for a show?

A· GARY INDIANA —— It's a gallery show at 356 Mission Road. Some photographs and videos. I'm going out to install it. There's also going to be an event co-hosted by Semiotext(e), who are reissuing several of my novels, where some people will be reading and talking about my work.

I've been shooting film portraits that are a little bit like the Warhol screen tests. A lot like them, really, but in colour, some with sound, some without – fixed shots that go on for five minutes. They're really fascinating. I set up one shot, the same as all of them, and the guy came in chewing a piece of gum, so I told him to keep doing that, and his mouth is just riveting, because there's no other motion in the frame. I've got about five people so far. I don't know how I'm going to present these things, whether I'll put them on a loop, or in light boxes. I've been making little films for a while. I'd really like to make a real narrative film, though maybe the time for me to do that has gone by. I'm showing *STANLEY PARK* also, the piece I had in the Whitney Biennial, and *KABATAS SCATTERED PICTURES*, a long video I shot in Istanbul and Ireland.

Q· THE WHITE REVIEW —— In 'Stanley Park', you turn a derelict prison's panoptic eye into footage of jellyfish and images of young, incarcerated Cuban men. In the piece on jellyfish you wrote for *THE FABULIST*, you wrote: 'It occurred to me that I had never seen an actual jellyfish. I thought I ought to film some, and put them in a movie I was making about a derelict prison complex on an island in southwest Cuba. The two subjects somehow belonged together.' Why do you think these subjects resonate with each other? Do jellyfish hold any symbolism for you?

A· GARY INDIANA —— I don't attach any symbolism to anything. I didn't think of convicts or prisons in connection to jellyfish except as visual elements of a picture. They ended up together in STANLEY PARK as a happy editing experiment. The only time you see 'young Cuban men' in the film is when two guys are drinking sodas and talking in a café; the only human figures you see 'in' the jail are very evanescent, overlaid images from gay porn movies, which mostly vanish almost before you register what they are. I wanted them to evoke the ghosts of prisoners who'd occupied these jails.

I shot some jellyfish footage in Toronto that turned out overexposed. A while later I shot the buildings and cell blocks in the Presidio Modelo. Afterwards I went to Vancouver and shot the jellyfish in the aquarium in Stanley Park. I'm not sure when I decided to combine them but that grew out of a fascination with the visual structures of these different things: the buildings as revolving Ferris wheels of claustrophobia and the jellyfish floating through them, beautiful in their way, except that most of their guts are trailing along in tendrils behind them. I combined very toxic aspects of life on this planet: surveillance and imprisonment on one hand, and this lethally parasitic organism that's reducing huge quadrants of the ocean biosphere to the texture of snot. I made the film as beautiful as possible, because beauty is quite often lethal.

Q. THE WHITE REVIEW — The narration of I CAN GIVE YOU ANYTHING BUT LOVE has an almost voyeuristic quality. It's as if you're as interested in withholding as you are in telling.
A. GARY INDIANA — I'm often interested in seeing how much I can remove from a story and still be able to tell it. A couple of years ago, I wrote and directed a playscript based on the Grand Guignol production of Octave Mirbeau's novel THE TORTURE GARDEN. It's

about this evil English whore, who lives in Shanghai and visits the prisons for the pleasure of watching violent tortures. Then she meets this French lieutenant aboard a ship, and gets him to desert, then proceeds to dominate him as his mistress. Later she takes him to the torture gardens where she has an orgasm. It's not a very good book, but reading the Grand Guignol script, I realised that the play was almost exclusively about this woman's cunt, and the way various men attempted to possess it. Not her, just her cunt. I took the script and crossed out all the language relating to colonialism — because that was implicit anyway — and just substituted words referring to her vagina, male and female genitals, and various sexual acts. I reduced the language as much as I could, down to something almost incomprehensible. I just told the actors, 'Imagine that all the words are there, but that your voice is a piece of magnetic tape that's been arbitrarily cut up.' It sounded like everyone was having a stroke. It's strange, because five or ten minutes into the play, you forget what the words mean. Everyone was saying things like 'cum', 'suck' or 'dong', but the words ceased to mean anything. People were just listening to these weird phonetics. That's not what I want to do with my writing, but it was an interesting experiment.

With the memoir, I simply took the attitude that I had no obligation to share everything about my life with some imaginary reader. This was no simple realisation, it took me a while to overcome the idea that I had to be in a literary confessional. I wanted only to be entertaining and brisk and thoughtful without oversimplifying anything. As far as withholding goes, I think that could only sound like an accusation in an era when people habitually spill their guts about everything, whether it's of any interest or not. Writing is as much about withholding as it is about telling. Believe me, you do not want a whole generation of Knausgaards.

Q· THE WHITE REVIEW — The way you structure *I CAN GIVE YOU ANYTHING BUT LOVE* relates to your early novels, like *HORSE CRAZY* or *GONE TOMORROW*, which mirror episodes in your own life. You compose the memoir as though it were a novel, creating a narrative that the genre might not allow.

A· GARY INDIANA — It's strange to me when someone states that a novel I've written mirrors my own life. Absolutely no one besides myself, in most instances, is in a position to say whether this is true or not. Quite often, it isn't, at least to the extent people claim. A person's life isn't a story. It just isn't. One of the main reasons I structured the book the way I did is because life doesn't make any narrative sense. Maybe it does after you die, but while you're alive, it really doesn't conform to narrative logic. It's not that I'm squeamish about sharing. I just didn't see any consistent form to my existence. I felt that I had to provide it with one, even if it meant imposing some kind of strict chronological form. But that's not what ended up happening; I found that doggedly following things in chronological order made no sense either. I made decisions based on aesthetic considerations. Was I really going to include the dreary months when I lived in Silver Lake with those horrible people – who might be interesting characters for a novel, but not for the story I wanted to tell? Or describe the seven boyfriends I had in succession in LA, instead of just condensing all that into the single, hot exterminator from the Valley, who was, after all, real? Dramatise my first trip to Cuba for no good reason? The years I spent in Boston? My *whole* life is not of interest, not in any blow–by–blow recounting of it,

and neither is anyone else's. I wanted to refine it, and focus on things that meant something, or could mean something by writing about them. Ergo, we never featured the words 'a memoir' in the book's title; I wasn't interested in documentary reality per se, and sometimes dispensed with it entirely to keep the book focused on the themes I had decided to explore.

Q· THE WHITE REVIEW — In *I CAN GIVE YOU ANYTHING BUT LOVE* you discussed being assaulted, twice. You write about the first instance early in the book, and you later tell Ferd that it wasn't as traumatic an experience as he might have believed it to be.

A· GARY INDIANA — I still don't know whether it affects you more, or affects you less when something like that happens to you when you're already on the edge, in a vulnerable state. The Hell's Angel who raped me held a knife to my throat, so I was more present for that until I passed out. But in the hospital, while the male nurse was raping me, I was already in a dissociative state, and I just left my body. I floated up to the ceiling. I looked down, and I could see it happening, but it didn't feel like it was happening to me. But I honestly don't know. Years later I read Doris Lessing's *BRIEFING FOR A DESCENT INTO HELL*, which is partly a mimicry of sub–acute schizophrenia, and it's the closest description I've found of the state I was in when I was raped by the nurse. The Freudian model is that you repress these things and thus they dictate your behaviour in a sort of Fu Manchu, subliminal way, without your knowing. But those stupid teenagers who hog–tied me and left me on a floating raft – another traumatic event in the book – I remembered that. I didn't ever suppress it. It wasn't a buried memory. What I've always wondered is: if you don't repress traumatic memories, if you remember things very clearly, does that make them more traumatic than things you repress, or less?

It's pretty clear from the book that I disassociate sex with somebody from loving someone as a person. In my own life, I've usually found it impossible to continue a sexual relationship with someone I've come to love and care about – although this has actually been a lot blurrier than the way I've represented it in the book. I don't think it has to do with being raped. It's probably the result of many things: the period in which I came of age, when homosexuality was still largely unspoken and unspeakable. It was mainly confined to bar ghettos in cities, and only 'liberated' by events like Stonewall in the sense that everybody suddenly felt free to fuck anybody they fancied in a gay bar without quite the same mutual revulsion.

I have a friend in Cuba. We're not sexually involved with each other, but we were. And for a time it developed into something like a marriage, and more recently settled into something less involving. I don't know. I mean, we're all very conditioned. Especially now, with gay marriage, people condition themselves into certain bourgeois expectations: how you live with another person, how you can be with another person, how exclusive that has to be, how circumscribed it has to be. People put all these rules on relationships. Intellectually, I just find that all to be asphyxiating.

Q· THE WHITE REVIEW —— Do you think that most people are preconditioned to feel jealousy?

A· GARY INDIANA —— I think we're deluged with narratives in which jealousy is mandatory for people in relationships. I was watching TV last night, and at least five shows were dramas about people in relationships sleeping with other people, getting found out, etc. It's everything; it conditions you It's funny at various periods in various cultures, there has been an understanding that sex is a rather frivolous activity, and isn't the be–all, end–all of human relations, or the common ground between two people who are already bonded in a very strong way. As long as people are nice with each other, I don't see why it makes a difference whether people are in a relationship or not. Because you see where it all takes people. We have this set-up of eight billion people, going on ten, at which point the earth becomes unliveable. So why should society support the ideology of endless growth and unlimited human reproduction? I mean, it's good to be with someone to help pay the mortgage, but the rest of it is either meaningless or pointlessly oppressive. It's artificial. It's all just consumerism; people call consumerism love. Jealousy is real enough, but not everybody has to feel it all the time, unless they're brainwashed.

I love the people close to me, intensely. But I know that being in love is a delusional fixation. You do things when you're in love that you could never do otherwise, but they're not necessarily good things. It's a kind of mania, and when I was younger I had it a lot. It never brought me anything good. You can't see people clearly when you're in love with them. You can't. I mean, it is good for some things. Francesco Clemente and I talked about this once. He said, 'When you're in love, the economy goes out the window.' This is true. If you're worried about money, falling in love will cure that – but only by making you dangerously indifferent to your actual problems. You don't think so much about money when you're in love, because you can only think about getting the loved one to love you back.

— Do these desires manifest in your work?

A· GARY INDIANA — *HORSE CRAZY* is all about an erotic obsession, carried on to the point of absurdity. It's a good subject for a novel. But I'm not the obsessive kind of artist that has the same menu of fixations in every book, if that's what you mean. In most of my books sexual or romantic desire is dealt with in a fairly derisory or satirical way. With visual work one usually pictures subjects that reflect some kind of desire, though it's usually a diffuse sort of longing for an erotics of life, rather than specifically sexual desires. In another sense, it's a question of editing: Why write the same novel twenty times? Why picture the same thing over and over? Do people have to think an artist is obsessed with something to take them seriously? I don't even understand why people think they must always have something in the works.

Q· THE WHITE REVIEW — Maybe it's what keeps some people going.

A· GARY INDIANA — Well, if that's keeping some people going, maybe there is something fundamentally wrong with their lives. In fact, I'm sure of it. Mind you, there's no such thing as a normal artist, we all just perform our pathologies in different ways. Typically, an obsessive writer writes the same novel every time, performs the same ritualised treatment of the same basic material, sometimes the result is good, sometimes it's terrible. I'm not that kind of writer.

Q· THE WHITE REVIEW — Do you really identify as a writer or an artist?

A· GARY INDIANA — After quite a few horrible experiences with the publishing industry, I no longer felt it was worth my time to engage with it on a regular basis. I had always done other things too, with photography, film, whatever. I'd avoided showing my visual work for many years because if you do more than one thing in the US, people don't know what to do with that, they don't know how to label you. And if you're comfortable doing nothing when you have nothing to say, that's regarded as something very strange, also. I don't identify with the image of the writer or the artist as a person tortured by an urgent need to express something. It's actually quite arbitrary whether you express something or not.

Q· THE WHITE REVIEW — When you do express something, is the satisfaction artificial?

A· GARY INDIANA — No, the process of making something is very gratifying. Actually, making something that takes as long as a book runs a gamut of emotional states, all very involving. Even in the immediate aftermath, when something goes out in the world, sometimes, if it gets a positive reception, or any reception at all, that can be satisfying in a different way. But I know very few artists, and very few writers, who don't go into a depressive tailspin after they've worked on something a long time and put it out into the world. If work itself has to be torture and the only pay off is how the public reacts, I'd rather not do anything.

MICHAEL BARRON, NOVEMBER 2015

WALKING BACKWARDS

BY

TRISTAN GARCIA

(*tr.* JEFFREY ZUCKERMAN)

'*Moderne, c'est déjà vieux.*' LA FÉLINE

I.

I pretended to remember and I smiled: it was time to tell the story once again.

A few hours before the concert, backstage at La Maroquinerie in the northern part of the twentieth arrondissement in Paris, I was smoking, legs crossed, sitting on a stool, in front of two freelancers for guitar magazines and three writers for French indie-rock sites. Our singer refused to talk to the press anymore, as if the press still existed. The tour promoter was selling us as part of a set of Californian rockers who had been famous in the eighties: a junkie who had survived the Paisley Underground scene was playing ahead of us, and after us would be a band we hadn't thought much of back then, a weird take on Camper Van Beethoven that had landed a Levi's jeans ad just before grunge took over. They'd written a hit, just like us, and we'd had plenty of fans. Right outside the concert hall, I'd seen a few fans already hanging around when I'd stepped out for a bit of air late in the afternoon. Guys my age, of course, but here, just like for the other tour dates around Europe, there would be some younger people. We'd been minor players in musical history, and there would always be teenagers who were into the also-rans rather than those who had made it. They're wrong, but I still have a soft spot for them.

Anyway, the story. In 1984, before going into the studio to record Wave Packet's second album, I came back to sleep at my parents' in Redwood City with my girlfriend at the time. The first album was terrible, hadn't sold at all, and I was scared as hell of flopping. The first time around, I'd been completely clueless, but now I knew. The compositions were weak. My dad, who was part Native American, told us about local tribes all around the bay and I got way too drunk. I fell asleep on the bed I'd had since I was a kid, with my fiancée in my arms. I was so young. On the floor by my nightstand I'd set up a little Philips recorder, since my room was in a shed far away from my parents' house, and that way when I felt like it I could play my guitar – back then it was a Rickenbacker I'd bought with the money from my first concert. When I woke up the next morning, hungover, I wanted to listen to what I'd composed over the last few days. I listened carefully and I was surprised to realise I'd gotten up in the middle of the night: my girlfriend hadn't heard a thing, but I'd been in some sort of trance and I'd recorded several minutes of a haunting melody that I'd tested later that day on the other guys in my band.

I crushed the butt under my heel while cracking jokes with the journalists. Much later, I would learn that Keith had composed the structure for 'Satisfaction' that same way, in his Carlton Hill apartment in St John's Wood.

My song was called 'Walking Backwards', and the title was my idea. For a long time, it hadn't felt particularly original, and I didn't feel like it was really mine, but it

worked. And then, over the course of all the concerts and interviews and album de-
luxe editions, my attention kept turning back to some part of this nicely put-together
song which had somehow stayed strong all these years. I loved it for that, and then I
hated it because I kept having to play it in front of crowds that didn't know anything
else I'd done, then I liked it again, because it was a nice reminder of that fame we'd
once had, of the best experiences we'd had in our lives, and then I got tired of it, and I
ended up totally indifferent. I wouldn't say that to the reporters interviewing me just
then, but that's the truth: I hear it, without any real feeling, and I know that's all that
will ever remain of me, long after everyone's forgotten what songs even were.

I tell the journalists the little story they already know. We were a post-punk
band, and like every other 'post-' movement that ever happened, we were jealous of
what we'd missed out on. I'd never been at the right place at the right time. I didn't
catch the Pistols at Winterland in 1978, or the Dead Kennedys at the Bay Area Music
Awards, or X, because they were in LA. I was 18 in 1980, and I wasn't aware of what
was going down just then in musical history, not the way I am now; I was just a kid
who had grown up by the airport in Millbrae, and even though I was just a few miles
away from San Francisco, I was a small-town kid. I've more or less stayed that way.
My mother, a nurse, raised me to be a nice, polite boy who folded his clothes and
did his homework on time. Then I became a teenager and we moved further south
to Redwood, and I met our singer, who had already lost his virginity. If you read an
article about us, you'll hear that we listened to the Velvets, Patti Smith, or Television,
just like everyone else. Actually, the music I knew best was what my mother loved:
variety, Bing Crosby, Dean Martin, a bit of jazz, Timi Yuro, and the scores for Henry
Mancini's movies. The bassist had been classically trained, and on Sundays he played
Ravel on the piano, but we kept up with the times thanks to 'Walking Backwards'.

After 1984 and the song's release as a single, we had two successful albums. We
toured abroad, and kept on regularly putting out a sort of jingling indie pop, the Byrds
played by boys in the eighties in baggy shirts with tousled hair. *NME* considered us
the American answer to the Smiths or Echo & the Bunnymen. The bands with the
Sarah or Postcard labels in Bristol and Glasgow, and Flying Nun in New Zealand,
called us their 'big brothers'. In retrospect, our best album, which Steve Lillywhite
produced, sounds terrible, especially the drums. It's too bad, but we never really
shaped the spirit of the times; it hovered like a ghost over all our compositions. The
album our fans like best came later, in 1988: it was pared-down, with a three-voice
harmony now that we had our new bassist, and harrowing melodies – our singer had
just divorced, I was listening to country music, and Merle Haggard and Charlie Rich
were playing on a loop on the tour bus. But there weren't any singles worth keeping,
and nothing good enough to make people forget 'Walking Backwards'.

The nineties were a mess for Wave Packet, and we split up at the end of the

F

decade, more or less on our last legs. Hip hop, electro... It was too late for us. And we'd come too early for the backlash: alt-country. The Jayhawks or Wilco, I met Green on Red, I produced The Fleshtones – but I didn't have the conviction they did. Nobody fought for our cause. We didn't have one; we wanted to follow movements. A bad album reminiscent of the Stones came out, with some boogie, and some gospel choirs, along the lines of Primal Scream's GIVE OUT BUT DON'T GIVE UP, then an abstruse, psychedelic CD much like what Kula Shaker was putting out just then, and then finally a stab at fusion with ridiculous electro bits jumbled in, to make people think we were still with the times. We had spent too much time in England, away from home, and we missed our rendez-vous with destiny. That was partly why some people liked us. I think we're held to be, by those who know us, the best of the average bands of our time. And 'Walking Backwards' is still on the radio. You'd definitely recognise it.

❡ Tonight's concert was OK. It was pretty clear what the audience thought of us. Not much attitude, no energy at all. Our singer has put on weight, and he looks like shit. We gave it our all, we were happy to play, but none of them really cared. Why would they, anyway? I take care of myself: grey-and-white hair, a whole afro of thick curls, a white jacket like the one Gram Parsons used to have, but without cannabis leaf or naked lady motifs. Simple, restrained. On stage, on a good day, I probably look like Lindsey Buckingham. I drop names and compare myself to them. But I can't help having all these names and songs in my head. I'm too self-aware. There's what I like, and then there's what I know. I know just about everything in rock these days. But I don't like anything much now.

Yawning, I headed back to the dressing rooms by myself, and decided to pop into the toilet.

Playing 'Walking Backwards' made me think about 1984 again, and that night, and my father who died ten years ago, and that girl who had also died since then, I think, and although I thought I'd been freed of that demon, now I was struggling with that question again: how the hell did I come up with that fucking song?

II.

In the hallway, a man yells out my name, explaining in some sort of primitive English that he has a blog, a name I don't get, and that he was a member of our fan club, ages ago. He's swallowing his words, spitting them out and stuttering, with convoluted phrases that he must have picked up while reading Chaucer alone in bed. He says he's a collector too, and claims we've corresponded by email.

Which isn't totally impossible. After I became a sound engineer, then a mixer, then a producer, I opened a tiny studio in the basement of my place on Potrero Hill.

Newish bands from the Bay area, and even San Diego and LA, came to see me. I know the entire scene, and I'm essentially a walking encyclopedia. Give me a short clip, and I swear I can identify it in one listen. For a long time, on Friday nights, I hosted a radio show, where I broadcast everything, or just about (I hate string quartets): garage bands, blue-eyed soul, deep soul, West Coast jazz, krautrock, Italo disco. I can tell right off if a new band's copying an old one, I can even figure out the way they're doing it, how much they've stolen, and through my website I'm in touch with collectors from around the world, so that I can pick up rarities.

It turns out this man had sold me some French psychedelic rock, something erotic by Philippe Nicaud, a single by Gérard Manset in Latin, or Esther Galil's 'Le jour se lève'.

Everyone apart from him has left the dressing room, and I decide to be patient. I suggest that he take a breather, sit down, give me a minute so I can piss, and then he can ask me all the questions he wants. His name is Jean-Luc Massenet. Like the composer of the 'Méditation' from THAÏS, I say. But he doesn't really hear me. It's only when I sit down in front of him and look at the mirrors bouncing his weird reflection around dozens of times that I realise he looks like one of those guys in front of a mall handing out flyers about the existence of aliens, and how the Lizard People are involved in the Iraq war, and Hitler's role in establishing Israel. His bright-orange ski jacket and Lester Bangs moustache made him look like a complete weirdo.

He explains that he teaches at a French middle school – which subject exactly I never quite hear, maybe English for French kids. He's out of breath, and wearing a zip-up sweater under his jacket. He's staring through his tortoiseshell glasses like a cow standing in a slaughterhouse doorway, or more like a kid who's always known that his very existence annoys everyone else. But I was polite; I got into rock music so I could hang out with freaks, and I'd feel dishonest now if I only spent time with good-looking freaks who smell nice and have minds as orderly as my mother's sock drawer.

There are people who don't know how to handle celebrity, but that's not my case – I know what I owe to the weirdest people who like me. So I offer him some whisky, he says he doesn't drink, so I pour us some tap water, which he seems to appreciate, and we make small talk.

He claims he's been trying to contact me for two months – and I cross my fingers that this madman, who seems to be in love with me or something, won't leave me bleeding from a hundred oyster-knife wounds. God knows we all get the Mark Chapman we deserve. But even though he looks at me goggle-eyed like I was a hero from the golden age of rock 'n' roll come down to earth to drink a glass of barely drinkable Paris tap water with him, soon he's only talking about himself, not Wave Packet. He wants me to listen to a tape he got from his uncle – and right this minute,

F

I have to admit I'm not paying attention to the specifics about his family. Something about his uncle being a small-time crook and a lover of good music, and Jean-Luc living a long way away with his parents on the island of Réunion. So apparently when he was growing up his uncle had sent him homemade cassette tapes on which he'd recorded himself making jokes, telling stories, sometimes playing a bit of music.

I don't really give a shit about his uncle, but I know how to listen with one ear without looking like I'm paying too much attention, or being rude. There's a specific sound within the vast array of throaty noises a human being can produce which indicates exactly the impression I want to give: what you're telling me is about as interesting as the weather forecast for the Galapagos, and you know it, but I'll listen anyway. A 'hmm-hmm' I can deploy expertly, mainly on the phone, with men and women alike.

From his huge fanny pack – for a second there I was sure he had a weapon stashed in it – he pulls out an old Korean-made cassette player. He's sweating even more heavily, his hands are clammy, and his English is getting less and less comprehensible. Then he pushes play and the empty room echoes with the far-off voice of a guy jabbering in French. Suddenly, in the background, a ghastly noise arises, and I can make out a rudimentary melody. Oh, I get it, ha-ha, it's 'Walking Backwards'. I wink at Jean-Luc. It's a kind of rustic version of my song, performed by his uncle. I say: 'He's got good taste.' But Jean-Luc is wringing his hands. Sure enough, the cover only goes on for a few more seconds before the tape stops. It seems like the poor guy was drunk, what with his singing out of tune and playing the guitar about as well as a caveman, but it's still pleasant enough. Refreshing, almost. So this uncle had sent a little cover version of my hit to his nephew, who still seems overcome by this gift.

'So is that how you became a fan?' I ask, to put him at ease.

'You don't understand,' he gulps. 'I found the tape three months ago, after my mother died. It was in her belongings up in the attic.'

'Oh.'

'My uncle died in 1981. The tape's from 1980. Four years before you sang the song.' A pause. 'And he's singing it exactly like you. He was the one who composed it! Do you know what I'm saying? It was him, not you.'

Fuck. I've been nice enough. He begins yelling in a high-pitched voice that I have to listen to this, come to his place... That I absolutely have to... Fuck! So that was his plan all along. He was going to ask me for the rights on behalf of his zombie uncle, who had been unjustly forgotten, who might have also composed 'Hey Jude', 'Billie Jean', and 'Seven Nation Army'.

So I start shouting right back at him: 'Go to hell, asshole.'

I can't believe this loser's managed to trick me. I walk out of the place boiling mad, grab my duffel coat, and go to meet everyone else at the restaurant nearby.

F

❡ I eat seafood and drink with people my own age, and we talk about what's new these days. My singer's completely clueless, and completely unashamed of it: nowadays, he only listens to Paul Quinn, Scott Walker, Roy Orbison, The Kinks, Johnny Rivers, and Billie Holiday. He's decided that everything made in the last two decades or so is worthless, that he shouldn't waste any time listening to feeble copies of the artists who invented everything. Rock is over, everything worth doing has been done already, all that's left is to remember it all – and kids these days can pull anything they want off the web, how do you expect them to make anything new? There aren't any gaps left, the world is full – and with that he pours himself some more Chinon red wine.

The programmer, who has taken the cap off his bald head, says no and waxes poetic about how 'promising little bands' and young people are still popping up on the California music scene and signing with major labels, like those clone-brothers Foxygen and Jacco Gardner, whose career paths we've seen a thousand times before. 'We're coming full-circle back to psychedelic rock, how exhilarating is that?' he says. Then he mentions a few French groups riffing off of old styles, but in a new way. After the third bottle of wine, I start getting snotty and asking everyone whether we're actually the ones who have gotten old, insisting we know about everything under the sun, or if it's just that times have changed, that our cultural moment prevents anything really *important* from taking place. But I get muddled up, sounding all philosophical, and the words just disappear from my head. They all listen to me politely anyway.

At the end of the table, a girl smiles at me.

❡ At the hotel, I didn't sleep.

After texting back and forth with the band manager, who had already left for Germany, I found out that we had a day off, but I was on my own. Slouched on top of the bedspread, I stared at a wine stain on the fuchsia-pink carpet that made me think of Mikhail Gorbachev's forehead. And I turned off the TV. I'd been married, I'd gotten divorced, I had a daughter, and I was in a relationship with a woman who didn't live with me. Soon, it would have been ten years since I'd stopped fooling around with girls, since my own daughter had become a teenager. My singer had taken the girl from the restaurant home. The bass player and the drummer were professionals who hadn't been part of the original group, and I had nothing in common with them apart from our job.

So I took my guitar out of its case, a Gibson Southern Jumbo from 1956 that I'd always kept nearby, and the old Korean-made cassette player fell out of the front pocket. Fuck. The cleaners had probably found it next to the instruments and assumed that it belonged to me. Just remembering Jean-Luc Massenet dripping with sweat was making my digestion even worse. I scowled.

I was still irritated by that dolt, and threw the tape into the trash. I sat down, and tried to start composing. Tunes came to me, covers, variations, nothing much more. And then, frustrated, I put down my guitar, crouched down to dig the tape out of the trash, and listened to it again. Only four or five minutes of the tape actually had the uncle's voice; the rest had been recorded over, with various performances on French national radio. These were long-forgotten English bands from the nineties, like Moose, The Auteurs, or Ride, but I recognised them all immediately. They didn't matter, though. I only cared about the uncle's bit. What was he saying in French? No clue. Maybe jokes meant for his nephew, like Lou Reed in TAKE NO PRISONERS, but in French and for a ten-year-old. Then he played some records. 'The House of the Rising Sun' – yeah, but I couldn't tell which version. Probably Frijid Pink, not The Animals or Bob Dylan or Lead Belly. Then a frenetic snippet from The Who's 'I Can't Explain'. Then 'Walking Backwards'. My song.

Shit, I thought, it really is my song. No question of it.

Because the uncle was talking over the music, and because the tape quality was pretty low, I had trouble pinpointing the actual source he was listening to. A cassette? A vinyl turntable? A four-track? After the fourth listen, I was half convinced that the versions of these three songs, including my own, weren't on any recording I knew of – not because of any lack of professionalism, since every time I listened they seemed more precise than I'd thought, but because I could make out some quality in the actual sound of the instruments, or in the mixing, that was nowhere to be found in any existing version. It was as if I was listening to Pete Townshend's original demo, or even the very first recording of 'Rising Sun Blues', before Lomax had ever touched it. And, more than anything, I felt like I was listening to my own tape, mysteriously recorded one summer night in 1984, in my parents' shed. But none of these three snippets, even mine, seemed to have been played with conventional instruments.

Worse still, I wasn't even sure that the uncle's 'I Can't Explain' had been played on a guitar; the crackle seemed more like it came from some unknown variety of lute, or from a seventeenth-century zither, but amplified, and in an unsettling way, as if there was no electricity. What was I actually listening to?

The more I listened to this five-minute sequence, the more obsessed I grew with these fragments of songs, each of which only lasted a few seconds. So I hit rewind ten times, twelve times, fifteen times, so that I could listen more closely to what, in a room that seemed to be Jean-Luc's uncle's kitchen, seemed to be my own song, a little slower than the original, passing briefly and spectrally through the sound spectrum, almost imperceptible but instantly recognisable.

By now, I was absolutely sure: it was a preliminary version of my song, mimicking the muffled sound of my Rickenbacker in my father's hut, and I almost felt like I could hear my fiancée sleeping beside me, in the night, when I was 22.

It was a nearly imperceptible five seconds resurfacing from my past.

III.

The next morning, I call Jean–Luc Massenet, after tracking down his number online. I apologise for having pushed him around, so I don't come off like a shitty rock star who thinks he can get away with anything, and especially since I haven't slept all night because I've been listening to the tape over and over, and I need to find out more about this fucking uncle.

He barely pays attention to my excuses and suggests that I come to his house. By now I'm pretty sure, or rather, I'm certain that he must be crazy, but I can't imagine leaving Paris without learning just how his uncle – or Jean–Luc himself – has re-recorded 'Walking Backwards' in its original, flawless perfection from the spring of 1984, and in a way that nobody has heard before, I think, besides my singer, because I'd lost my Philips recorder and the accompanying tape several months later, when my girlfriend had dumped me and the band had left for Seattle.

He gives me the address for his mother's house, which had been his uncle's first but now belonged to her, in Le Plessis–Robinson, a suburb south of the city. I take a cab there; it's a nice summer day, even though the sky over the Plessis streets is as grey as the stone of the buildings. On the hillside, east of the city, the cab stops in front of an old stone–built place on the edge of the woods. The air is clear, and under the plane trees I feel like I'm stepping back in time, peering over all of Paris from a sloping road, like back when the area was covered in forest. The chatty driver had explained that Le Plessis–Robinson was a new town, barely a century old, that it had originally been called Le Plessis–Liberté during the revolution. The house, off to the side, must have already been standing back then. I grope around for a doorbell besides the entrance, but all I can find is a little bell. A minute later, Jean–Luc Massenet, wearing an argyle cardigan over his shirt, runs through the overgrown garden and opens the gate.

'Hello.'

He lets me in, hurriedly shows me into the house, and offers me a glass of milk. He's still talking in a barely comprehensible English. He's caught a cold and keeps blowing his nose into a bit of tissue that he subsequently stashes in the sleeve of his shirt – a detail that makes me sorry I've bothered to come. The whole house is glum and dim. Loose tiles fill the floor of an empty, barely furnished hallway. In the rooms on both sides of the hall are several too–high mirrors that just reflect my host's bald scalp, and the fireplaces are all boarded up. I clear my throat and notice, to my surprise, that the place's acoustics are splendid, notwithstanding the cold. With the palm of my hand I touch the damp walls, and I say some nice words about the building to Jean–Luc, who brings me my milk on a plastic plate with an image of Sly and the Family Stone on it. Looking up towards the back room, I notice his mausoleum. Whereas the other rooms are empty, and only have one or two chairs that need reup-holstering, this one is packed to the gills with shelves overflowing with vinyl records,

its walls covered with posters and framed displays, its floor cluttered with crates of
fanzines. Straight through the doorway is a massive photo of me, from 1984, laughing,
besides my singer. Jean–Luc goes red, apologises.

'Don't worry about it.' I look around; I'm used to seeing the places neurotic collectors keep. But he interrupts me, so that I can confirm the order in which he should
keep his pile of bootleg recordings from the Cosmic Christmas session of THEIR
SATANIC MAJESTIES REQUEST next to the VHS tape of RETURN TO WATERLOO and a
reproduction of the Roaring Twenties–style painting that decorates the sleeve for The
Country Hams' 'Walking in the Park with Eloise'.

'Wait, I think this will be interesting for you.'

I had come for the tape, but I still look at what he wants to show me. The excitement in his voice makes me suspect that he had planned out everything – more or less
skilfully – so that I would see *this*.

'What is it?'

Beneath the record sleeve for JOURNEY THROUGH THE PAST, at the bottom of the
shelf, he carefully pulls out a small trunk, about two feet wide and one foot tall.

'My mother kept the tapes that Uncle Jacques sent me. She died this winter. I
found this trunk in the attic. It must have survived the fire.'

'The fire?'

'Uncle Jacques died in a fire in this house in 1980. Didn't I tell you?' He got up,
opened a wooden door at the back of the room, and gestured for me to poke my head
in. The entire back wall of the shack was ruined: the walls were crumbling, darkened,
covered in weeds, the roof was sinking, and what must have been especially important considering this massive, beautiful house, was out in the open, right by the ash
and maple trees. He lived there.

'Have a look.'

He had walked back to the trunk and opened it. I was expecting to see other tapes,
or even artisanal instruments that the Massenets had invented. But no. There was
nothing there, practically nothing, at the bottom of the case. Piles of music magazines,
the RECORD MIRROR and the MELODY MAKER, a few unimportant EPs, some personal papers, and two wooden rollers. Jean–Luc Massenet picked them up carefully
and handed them to me: 'So what do you make of these?'

'Ehrm, they look like wax cylinders for a phonogram, but made of oak. Maybe
they're sculptures?'

He pointed at the circular end of the roller, on which a name had been carved:
Constantin Sélène. Then I looked more closely: the wax cylinder was invented in
1887 – or maybe a few years earlier – by Edison. But we were dealing with a rather
heavy item made out of wood, lacquered with a strange substance, a glaze I wasn't
familiar with, pretty hardy, solid, almost rough. I caressed the object. Threads went

F

around the entire outer surface of this cylinder, about eight inches in diameter, about two times as long. I counted more than twenty grooves in just a quarter of an inch. I had never seen anything like it.

Jean–Luc's excitement was palpable. 'See? Do you see?'

Some kind of acoustic recording on the wood. 'Who's Constantin Sélène?' He didn't know.

'All right.' I set down the first roller. 'What does this have to do with your tape, and my song?'

He frowns. 'You haven't figured it out?'

'No.'

'My uncle, on the tape, told me that he was going to play me some nice old music. Then he put on "The House of the Rising Sun". Then The Who. Then your song. And the whole time he was talking about the record he was playing. It's a wooden roll.' He points at the cylinder. 'Your song was recorded on it. By Constantin Sélène.'

¶ First, I said I needed a bit of fresh air. The sweat, the humidity, the musty odour of his rock 'n' roll mausoleum – I thought I would pass out. As I made my way through the ruins behind the house, smoking a Marlboro, I started to feel a bit better. This whole place, and this guy, seemed kind of psychedelic and mesmerising and morbid, and this was all making me worry I might go crazy the same way he already had. But once I was outside, in front of the scrim of trees swept through by the spring winds, with a cigarette dangling from my lips, I could get my thoughts in order.

I rubbed my stubbly cheeks, and scraped the grey pebbles under my boots.

'I'll buy them.'

'What?'

'The trunk, the cylinders, all of it.'

He smiled. 'I knew it.'

'What do you mean?'

'You know,' he said quietly, 'that doesn't change anything. My uncle still composed "Walking Backwards" before you. And Constantin Sélène composed it before him and recorded it on wood cylinders. Maybe it flowed through me. I was just a kid, but I heard this song on the tape he sent me when I was living in Réunion, four years before you wrote it. And that's why I always liked your band: it's partly because of me that the hit ever happened. I was a cosmic conduit.'

I didn't say anything back; I exhaled.

I would have liked to explain to him that I remembered when and how I'd created 'Walking Backwards', found the chords, invented the title, and then this bridge, which was what really made the song, but he knew as much as I did that it was all a lie. He knew the story.

F

'Well, are you going to find a way to play the wooden rollers?'

'How much?'

I crushed the butt with my heel.

'Money, you mean? Nothing.' He seemed scared, or shocked. 'I'm not blackmail-ing you.' All he wanted was a signature on his original Wave Packet poster from circa 1984.

Then I called a cab. We drank one last glass of milk. I loaded everything in the car trunk. By six in the evening I was in Roissy, with the singer, and the girl from the night before, who was crying.

I stopped thinking about it. I played 'Walking Backwards' forty-seven times in a row, from Bremen to Athens. We made a bit of money. Now that everybody down-loaded music, our income from this song had gone way down, and that was why we'd had to go back on the road even though we were in our fifties.

The business just isn't what it used to be.

IV.

When I got back to San Francisco, I found the trunk waiting for me in my studio. It had been there for ten days already. For the next month, I didn't have any bands to produce. I was exhausted, purposeless, I felt emptied out the way I always do at the end of a tour. My girl had left for Asia to get a stupid MBA, telling me the whole time that the East would be the future.

Through the bay window on the fourth floor of my house, at the top of Potrero Hill, near the square where the bums camped out at night, I could make out the hills of Twin Peaks, and the Bay. I lived alone, but I spent my days working with Joey, my as-sistant, in the basement and on the ground floor. I drank a glass of white port, my bare feet propped up on the couch, and watched the city light up like a thousand cigarettes while I pulled tight a jacket exactly like the one Arthur Lee had worn on the back of DA CAPO. Then I walked down to meet Joey and opened the trunk in front of him.

'What do you make of this?'

'Well, just looking at it,' he said, 'it's a box made of oak and leather, with some iron braces.' Joey searched for a few similar boxes on Google Images, and said that it probably came from the eighteenth century, before Louis Vuitton had invented flat lids. We joked about Jay-Z, Kanye West, and Louis Vuitton suitcases. I was really fond of Joey, a promising young guy who could keep his mouth shut. He had a reced-ing chin and a man-bun, and he looked down at his generation's music idols, and the way people his age behaved. He was wasting his potential already by sharing my tastes and ideas of what rock should be. He was ten times cleverer than I had been at his age, and I often reminded him that if we'd met in 1984, when I was the same age he is now, he would have decided I was a cretin and wouldn't have wanted anything to do with me. But I was 53 years old, and we got along well, so I let him hang out with me and listen to republished recordings of Margo Guryan, Billy Nicholls, and Del Shannon, or make mixtapes of 'All-Time Best Performances' on old CD–Rs using songs by Mann and Weill, or Leiber and Stoller, or Barry and Greenwich – instead of finding himself a girlfriend.

I whiled away that first night smoking weed with Joey, thinking about art and some way of constructing a way to listen to the wooden cylinder. I didn't bother telling him about 'Walking Backwards' on the Massenet tape, because I was stupidly ashamed of evoking my imaginary imposture, and the idiotic idea that I'd plagiarised a Frenchman from Le Plessis-Robinson. So I simply told him that maybe, just maybe this was a kind of acoustic recording contemporaneous with wax cylinders from the end of the nineteenth century, and that a family may somehow have kept up the tradition through to the eighties. Which, in and of itself, would have been a sufficiently important discovery for sound engineers like the two of us. Joey was the one to notice that one of the cylinder's ends was damaged, and didn't have any grooves or furrows like those on the rest of the two cylinders. Maybe I was a bit stoned when I decided to slice a sliver off the two cylinders for analysis. The next day, once I was sober, I went to visit one of my nephews, who was finishing up his studies at the Stanford Archaeology Center. When I showed him the varnished wood, he hummed and suggested that I talk to the specialists at a dendrochronology lab at Cornell, who would know how to analyse European wood.

Dendrochronology, I would come to learn, is a way of dating wooden objects based on tallying a tree's annual rings, since those appear consistently. In our hemisphere, trees grow from spring to the end of the summer, and each year they accumulate a new growth ring, separated by lighter circles of wood each spring, as the sap rises. By using complex calendars that had been created by checking data for a particular geographical area and tracking variations in weather, my nephew said, scientists could determine a tree's death to the nearest year.

'But what if the tree was cut down long ago, and it wasn't carved until just now?'

'The wood was varnished. I don't know what this material is, but air bubbles have probably been trapped in the varnish. If you use carbon-14 dating, you can verify the date the artefact was created.'

But I would have to wait three months.

The first month, Joey and I spent all of our time inventing various contraptions. It felt like being Edison, only *backwards*: we had a recording, and we needed a machine not to make the recording, but to read it. Joey wasn't convinced, after examining the grooves, that there was music recorded on it, but he went along with me anyway, out of sheer curiosity. A mica diaphragm turned out to be too small to amplify the vibrations a needle made while moving between the wood's threads: we came up with a new one that was abnormally big. Then we had to test the springs: unfortunately, as we put together the hub, outer hook, and knob, we couldn't do much with the stiff wood. We needed something that would be both more sensitive and more robust.

And then the traditional needles hadn't worked. Sometimes they ruined the varnish, sometimes they broke. Joey tried everything he could possibly think of. And I painstakingly reconstructed a phonograph adapted for a full cylinder. I carefully selected a membrane connected by the spring and the stylus to the needle which, as it passed over the hills and valleys of the roller's grooves at a consistent speed, tugged at the arm. I was hoping that, coming and going this way, the membrane would emit waves into the surrounding air that replicated the ones the Frenchmen had engraved in the wood. I'd also put together a frustoconical mandrel to hold the shaft we'd bolted to the end of the cylinder, and come up with a system for adjusting the speed by using a lever, because I wasn't sure of the rotation speed the roller was adapted to.

Despite all these efforts, it was impossible to read this varnished wooden cylinder: we couldn't find a suitable needle.

After a month, we had to get back to work, what with all the bookings that local bands had made for the studio, so Joey had to set this aside. I took our silly homemade phonograph up to the fourth floor, and kept it on the coffee table in my living room, where I had a view of the sleeping city, and I put the two wooden cylinders behind the glass doors of my bookcase.

¶ Two months later, my nephew emailed me and suggested that we get a drink on Valencia Street. He told me that his colleagues at Cornell had been fascinated by the circular piece I'd sent them, and they'd been able to determine a precise date for the wood.

'Well?'

It was a sample from 1813.

I was dumbstruck. Sixty years before phonographs and wax cylinders had been invented; before the first electric dynamo even existed.

'1813? Really? Are you sure?'

He nodded. 'And the carbon–14 testing confirms that the varnish is less than two centuries old. The people I know were asking where you dug it up. It didn't look like a fragment of furniture, despite the lacquer from the time.'

'What lacquer?'

He patiently explained that in the eighteenth century Far Eastern lacquers had become fashionable among European royalty and that the East Indian Companies had brought back entire boats full of Chinese luxury furniture – but this piece from 1813 was made of wood directly from Europe and lacquer from Asia, although the

Europeans didn't know yet how to make it. That was what had puzzled the archaeologists: the varnish had been put by the Europeans on the circular fragment that I'd sent them, and in an unusual way.

'How come?'

'It looks like the lacquer was applied once, and then polished repeatedly, several years later, by *another object covered with the same varnish*, maybe to smooth out the surface.'

❡ From that point on, I didn't talk about this with anyone. I made up a lie for my nephew, and I told Joey that the item was a fake that was only 20 or so years old.

Then I feverishly started seeking out sap from the Chinese lacquer tree, a blend of urushiol, resin, and albuminoids, which I bought one evening from a Chinatown dealer. This varnish matched the outer layer of varnish applied to the wood of my cylinder.

When I was by myself in the living room at night, I dipped a very long medium-thickness needle in the bubbling paraffin, applied it to the Chinese lacquer, and let it harden. The solution had been a simple one, but it had escaped both Joey and me: we had to cover the needle with a varnish identical to the one that coated the grooves, after which I set the lacquered needle on the stylus and, at three in the morning, as I sat nervously with dishevelled hair and wearing nothing but underwear and a wife-beater, drinking rum by the glass, I carefully positioned the small shaft of the cylinder in the mandrel. I waited a minute, moved the needle, adjusted the rotation speed with the lever, and ever so slowly set the tip of the varnished needle deep in the groove that wound in a spiral from the end of the roller.

Then I turned the sound all the way up.

And I listened, rapt, to music from the year 1813.

V.

Even as I listened to it for the first time, I knew what was wrong.

I was sweating heavily and during the four minutes that the cylinder had played, I'd felt more and more sick. I couldn't quite figure the different pieces at first, because the only thing that could be heard was a long, hazy stream of sound, where every melody blurred into the next one like foam in water; but I already knew all the components of this two-hundred-and-fifty-second ocean. And it very clearly wasn't classical music, or traditional songs from the eighteenth century.

What the hell. This was funk music. Glam rock. Reggae! Doo-wop! Even techno. In 1813.

By some kind of miracle, mechanical equipment and instruments from that time were putting out a set of sounds exactly like the ones that, more than a century later, came out of Roland TR 808 and Yamaha synths and Fender Stratocasters and all sorts of different electric amps.

My blood was running cold.

Then I played the cylinder again, with a pencil in my hand and a spiral notebook ready to write in. The second time through, I recognised six pieces from the twentieth century. The third time, seven more. By the fifth listen, the list was complete.

This is how I ultimately summed all this up: one or more men from the early nineteenth century, Constantin Sélène certainly among them, had engraved some sort of prophetic mixtape, foreseeing everything down to the exact note and sound, and using completely analogue media (not electronic or even electric) to make at least nineteen of the most innovative – although not necessarily famous – snippets of popular music recorded in the twentieth century.

I heard a French man from two centuries ago perform, with each sample varying in length and intensity, this sequence: 'When the Saints Go Marching In', in the version Louis Armstrong had performed in the thirties; 'Livery Stable Blues'; 'Body and Soul' with Coleman Hawkins; 'The Preacher'; the main theme of *BIRTH OF THE COOL*, later played by the nine musicians Miles Davis had brought together; the start of Ornette Coleman's 'Free Jazz' B side; The Damned's 'New Rose'; 'Rocket 88'; The Turbans singing 'When You Dance', where the syllables 'doo–wop' were heard for the first time; 'Out of Sight', played by James Brown; the first bit of ska Prince Buster ever made; the refrain from 'Ride a White Swan'; Brian Eno's 'Big Ship'; 'I Can't Explain' by The Who, which I had already heard on Jean–Luc Massenet's cassette tape; 'Five Miles High' by The Byrds; Kraftwerk playing 'The Robots'; 'On & On', the very first Chicago house record; Carl Craig's 'Bug in the Bassbin'; and the shoegaze song 'You Made Me Realise'.

I reread what I'd written in the notebook, and was taken aback. It was filled with instants from the origins of various genres and movements, musical pieces that had been considered radically new or ahead of their times. But performed between one and two hundred years early – and *carved into solid wood*.

What the fuck was going on?

¶ I sighed heavily as I took out the first cylinder and inserted the second one, and what I feared came to pass.

For the first ten seconds that the second roller played, I could hear, fully and clearly, the riff from 'Walking Backwards'. My crowning achievement, created in 1813, barely two years before Waterloo, and reproduced in the original, unadulterated form I'd conceived of one beautiful summer night in Redwood City.

F

¶ The possibility that I'd gone crazy definitely crossed my mind. I couldn't possibly think that a Frenchman from Napoleonic times had not only created rock 'n' roll, and all that came before, and after, by himself, without any electricity, but also performed these pieces using lutes, gitterns, some plucked-string instruments, a prepared piano, drums, and trumpets, and then subsequently found a way to record acoustic house music on a bit of oak.

Around dawn, I burned a .wav file from the first cylinder onto a CD and started visiting various friends in the San Francisco music and radio industry to do a blind test. Not all of them had my encyclopedic knowledge of every genre and every style, and so none of them could recognise every single one of the nineteen clips, but they were all able to immediately identify at least a third of the pieces, especially those that hewed most closely to their personal tastes, whether jazz or rock or electronic music. As I tallied everything up, I was able to get five or six definite confirmations for each sample. So I wasn't just projecting my overly extensive knowledge on this wretched bit of wood. Most of my friends insisted that the short snippets I'd played were some-what exotic, but couldn't decide whether these were clever remakes by avant-garde artists in New York or rudimentary versions by hare-brained rock music lovers on a Tongan island.

VI.

I holed myself up, fired Joey, and cancelled all the bookings for my studio.

Both my singer and the Wave Packet manager tried to get in touch with me. They were hoping to record an album since the Europe tour had gone so well, but I pushed back the deadline and focused all my energy on researching Constantin Sélène.

I studied the trunk carefully, and after I'd prodded and poked every square inch of the leather, I ended up finding a sewn-up patch beneath the lid, which contained a single, yellowing piece of paper: Constantin Sélène's record of service as a soldier of the Napoleonic Empire.

I was eating too little and drinking too much. I didn't get dressed until noon, when I would run a few errands down the street, and spent my nights flicking through books and documents from that era online. I wrote to a specialist who taught at Santa Barbara, and ended up learning that Constantin Sélène had been mentioned in SOUVENIRS D'UN SOLDAT DE L'EMPIRE, by a man named Maupetit. On the pages that my correspondent had scanned, I saw that he had served under General Junot from 1807 to 1808, and was involved in the invasion of Portugal. They had entered by Castela Branco, and gone through Abrantes, and then he and his fellow soldiers were hampered by torrential rains over the mountains of the Beira Alta and Beira Baixa provinces, and consequently abandoned by the other troops. Whereas some of them, left to their own devices, plundered the nearby villages during the thunderstorm, Sélène was taken in by an old monk, a certain Fernando Paiva. When the regular troops, including Maupetit, went back through the city on their way home, Sélène vouched for Paiva, and apparently this testimony saved the clergyman from summary execution. But this turned out to be in vain, because the old man died of natural causes in the following weeks. The soldier Sélène came back to France a changed man: wild–eyed, sustaining a flesh wound, and carrying an old chest that he never let out of sight at any time of day or night.

Then Sélène left the army and moved to Le Plessis–Liberté, far from the chaos in Paris during Napoleon's Hundred Days. I can certainly imagine what he was doing during these last ten years of his life, because he died in 1823, during the Restoration – his death certificate, which I requested from the local city hall, was still kept in the municipal archives. He had died when his house caught fire.

¶ After so long without any exercise, I'd put on some weight. I'd been living miserably, glued to my computer screen. Bent over my old iBook, I got back in touch with Jean-Luc Massenet, who had some news about his uncle on his mother's side. He had been told that Jacques Massenet had bought Sélène's suitcase in London during the sixties, where he was 'doing business' right before the blues boom and the British Invasion. The other uncle had looked through the suitcase long ago: he claimed that he'd found dozens and dozens of wooden cylinders, which he'd assumed at the time were abstract–art statues, thinking that Jacques had been dealing art on the sly, which perhaps wasn't entirely untrue.

Carved on the circular lower end of my cylinder was the number 117. Now I had confirmation that at least a hundred other cylinders had been engraved by Sélène, but I was careful in what I told Massenet about the contents of the rollers. In every email, I claimed that the grooves just held simple folk music, like nursery rhymes for babies drawn from traditional French folklore at the time. When Massenet asked me to send him a copy of the recording, I did a performance myself of a little ditty from the start of the nineteenth century, 'Pauvre Jacques', using some sheet music I'd dug up online, and I sent him a .mp3, but not before I'd thoroughly reprocessed and aged the sound of my performance in every way I could think of. I chuckled at the thought that I could fool him so easily. I'd grown particularly possessive and uneasy at the idea that other people might have some knowledge of this secret.

And when, as I was skimming through a long rumination written on a music blog, I came across this photo of Alexis Korner, who had mentored every white kid who'd gotten into the blues in London during the early sixties, from the Rolling Stones to Eric Clapton, from Eric Burdon to Long John Baldry, a feverish shudder went through my body: on the low table, behind Alexis Korner, next to his guitar, there it was.

A wooden cylinder.

Three days later, I found a second one, on a shelf behind Ramblin' Jack Elliott, the man who claimed to have gotten Bob Dylan started. And a third one in a promo photo of The Pretty Things, shortly before *S. F. Sorrow* came out.

So the jig was up. They all knew, every one of them. The ones who had made history for jazz, folk, rock, hip–hop – each of them had found one of Constantin Sélène's cylinders, and found a way to decipher them, if not in full then at least a small portion: with this small bit of music, sometimes just a few seconds, they had built entire careers, oeuvres, and blazed new trails in every subsequent decade. Duke Ellington, Jimi Hendrix, Marley Marl... they'd all copied Constantin Sélène.

None of them were any more gifted than you or me, but they'd all had the good luck of *finding it*.

After I noticed a cylinder beneath the elbow of James Gurley, the former guitarist for Big Brother who had died five years ago and whom I'd known a bit, I called his wife, Margaret, who still lived in Palm Desert. Once I sent her my description, she immediately recognised what I was talking about. James had kept it as a totem of his first acid trips from back when he was a hippie. When I asked her if James had 'extracted' any music from it, she seemed thoroughly astonished. 'Some vibrations, maybe.' But he had never done anything but look at it and touch it: 'Goodness,' she said, 'it was just a bit of carved wood, some kind of Indian artwork.' I asked where it was now. She didn't have the least idea. As far as she knew, James had gotten it from Chet Helms, the larger–than–life promoter of the San Francisco Sound, who had met Janis Joplin at the University of Texas at Austin, before coming here to California. In his later years, Chet had set up a gallery and become a prominent art dealer. An older member of the Dog Family I'd worked with to make an album honouring all the Haight–Ashbury veterans knew the whole story behind the statue. It was presented to Chet by a beatnik, who himself had been given it by an African–American man from New Orleans before the war.

The more I learned about various rock figures who'd known about the cylinders, the more I felt hoodwinked. I'd believed in legends, heroes, and inventors, but as I came to realise that I was the only one, perhaps the first one, aside from Jean–Luc's uncle, to see and hear the rollers for what they actually were, the more powerful I felt as a keeper of the truth.

I was almost transfixed by joy when I randomly came across the mention of a certain Louis Sélène in a Louisiana newspaper from 1860, *The New Orleans Bee*. I was eventually able to confirm that he was in fact Constantin's great–nephew. He had been a French explorer come to try his luck in the former French colony, after the territory had been sold to the United States. As he lived near French refugees from Saint–Domingue and the Louisiana Creoles, Louis Sélène seemed to have been

F

influenced by the black slaves, soon to be emancipated, who had danced bamboulas, and who learned from him how to play brass instruments in a local band.

So it had all come from Sélène, after all.

His great-nephew had inherited what remained of the cylinders after the fire that had killed Sélène, and brought the suitcase to the United States in 1860, to where American black music had been born. A suitcase that reappeared a century later in London, during the era of The Beatles and The Rolling Stones, whereupon the uncle acquired it, doubtless because he bought and sold artworks.

The story was starting to take shape, but my eyes were starting to hurt. I needed glasses. I had neglected myself, and I knew it. As I looked in the bathroom mirror, I thought momentarily that I was starting to look more and more like Jean-Luc Massenet. It crossed my mind that he'd known from the very beginning. That he'd listened to the cylinder too. And that he'd wanted to get rid of it all. So that I would go mad instead of him. I hadn't had any response from him by instant message, or email, or phone for several days.

He had disappeared.

¶ I decided to stop for a moment in my hunt for the truth.

With a clean-shaven face, I strode up and down San Francisco's streets, and went to visit Joey so I could apologise for my strange behaviour over the previous months. He'd found a girlfriend, stopped smoking so much weed, had cut his hair short, and stopped obsessing about sixties music. Then I went to buy my old singer a drink and talked to him about the forthcoming album. The sounds I heard in supermarkets, on the docks, at my friends' houses, everywhere, seemed unreal and spoke to me with a voice that I imagined belonged to Constantin Sélène, the French soldier, which in turn reproduced the old Portuguese monk's.

As if I now knew the origin of all things, I smiled indulgently at the pop culture of today and of yesteryear. Forgive them, for they know not what they do, Elvis no more than Taylor Swift or Rihanna. They're all singing the old Portuguese monk's music. Good or bad, genius or impostor – I forgave them all indiscriminately.

Walking out of my singer's house, I got a call from Margaret, James Gurley's widow, who told me that her husband had gifted the 'statuette' to some Mexican Native Americans during a trip there shortly before his death. But the Native American communities were falling apart. And so I found the 'statuette' circulating online among various resellers, on the Baja California black market, for practically nothing. It was being given away for less than ten dollars: twenty original masterpieces of human musical culture, for the cost of a Tex-Mex lunch. That was how the market worked. As I zoomed in on the seller's image, I thought I could make out the number 25 carved on the bottom of the damaged cylinder.

F

❡ I checked my mailbox when I came back, and found that the New Orleans municipal archives had sent me a copy of several rare issues of *THE NEW ORLEANS BEE* featuring two excerpts from a long *'poème d'imagination'* signed by Jules Sélène. In clipped language, the great–nephew of the soldier Constantin seemed to be telling, under the guise of fiction, the story of his ancestor. A zydeco musician I'd met ten years earlier while recording *N'AWLINZ: DIS DAT OR D'UDDA* helped translate several portions, and I was able to get this story out of the poem: a French soldier meets a Franciscan monk, who saves his life and tells him his secret: he has transcribed onto hundreds and hundreds of musical scores, using a new system of musical notation, 'the music of original Nature', which he received in a revelation. As death approaches, Paiva gave the young Frenchman his treasure: not just thousands of melodies that remained untranscribed, but also the designs for various machines to reproduce the sounds of 'the original Nature of things' and to intensify them.

So the prose poem became a strange *TOMORROW'S EVE* in Creole.

The Frenchman returned to his homeland and dedicated himself to organising and engraving this great original music into wood, but he went mad, set fire to the sheet music, the machines, the engravings, and only a single suitcase had escaped the blaze.

The exact reason that the Frenchman had gone insane was difficult to determine, because Louis Massenet's text was especially circumspect in this respect. But it would seem that in Paris, at a debut performance of the final masterpiece of 'the greatest composer of his time' (which could have possibly been Beethoven, and therefore his 'Große Sonate für das Hammerklavier', Opus 106), he heard a note–for–note replication of a fragment from one of the monk's musical scores.

And so I took it that he had realised that 'the original music' was in fact 'the music to come'; that he wasn't currently retranscribing the Lord's first songs, but the long and laboured saga of human centuries to come; and I think that the French veteran couldn't bear to hear the future, and had opted to reduce these papers and far–seeing machines to ashes and embers.

❡ The day after the next, I received the roller numbered 25 from Tijuana.

I was less shaky and less excited than the first two times. I started playing the cylinder, which I had already cleaned and restored, on my phonograph. And I recognised a bit of MPB, Ethiopian jazz, Mahmoud Ahmed's 'Erè Mèla Mèla', some bluegrass, some trance, some dubstep, and plenty of Californian psychedelia. It was all instantly familiar, as I'd thought it might be. Except for one section. Not much, really, but a stretch of nine measures at most, that didn't sound familiar at all. I played it again. Still nothing. Maybe Asian music? I looked through my shelves of vinyl records, but I couldn't find anything just then.

F

¶ A week from now, we were supposed to do several recording sessions at a studio for the new Wave Packet album. I asked Joey to come along to help with the production. The singer was harassing me, asking for a demo. But my head was completely empty except for the unidentified nine–measure sequence from the twenty–fifth cylinder.

So that I could get it out of my thoughts, I started researching the monk Fernando Paiva, although I didn't expect much. To my great surprise, I found out that the Stanford University archives had several biographical details about him. He had accompanied the conquistador and governor of Alta California, Gaspar de Portolá, at the end of the eighteenth century, and for ten years he had stayed in contact with a small tribe of Native Americans by the bay, who were quickly killed off by various illnesses. There were no survivors left by the time he left to return to Europe.

This tribe, which seemed not to have had a name, had lived in the heights of what is now Palo Alto – and Redwood City.

My God... My hometown. Everything came from there.

I felt dizzy. In the poorly lit stacks of the Stanford library, amid thousands upon thousands of books, almost exactly where, two and a half centuries earlier, Fernando Paiva had met my father's forebears' forebears, I could almost make out, with the dread and awe of a man who, upon reaching the uppermost heights of heaven, realised that he was actually underground, in hell, Native Americans who could have been either smiling or grimacing, crow's feet at the corners of their eyes, carving cylinders with clay, their feet bare and their skin suntanned, busy carving furrows in the clay with their long nails, all the while chanting the complete works of Beethoven, Schoenberg, John Coltrane, The Beatles, and – above all – my own song.

I stopped looking, and stopped my fall down the centuries–deep abyss, towards the origin of all things.

VII.

By the time spring came, I had almost managed to forget Sélène, Paiva, and the Native Americans who kept reappearing in my nightmares every so often, but I was still obsessed with the nine measures that I'd never heard before. I'd grown terribly suspicious, and didn't let myself play the arresting sequence to Joey, or to any of my friends who loved music. After spending the day at the studio, I'd go up to my fourth–floor living room, and gulp down bottles of cheap Australian wine, rip–offs of French varietals made in Victoria, while carefully and systematically listening to everything similar I could think of. Sometimes, a short break in one obscure CD or another would slightly approximate the rhythm and melody of my mysterious snippet, and I'd try to convince myself that I'd found it once and for all. But an hour later, I'd have to concede that the other snippets carved into the cylinder had never been embryonic approximations of a song; on the contrary, they'd been the very essence, such that the music inscribed in Constantin Sélènc's rollers had always been more faithful to the snippets executed in the twentieth century than the snippets themselves. And that wasn't the case here. So I'd get back up from my futon, and continue my search in the living room.

My partner had left me, and Joey said that I'd gotten completely unbearable. He was very much in love; his girlfriend had domesticated him thoroughly. I became the bachelor he no longer was; I didn't like anybody or anything, I was snobby about everything and nothing, and totally self-contradictory. Worst of all, the Wave Packet sessions were coming up soon, and I didn't even have the beginnings of a melody to give them. I'd gotten bitter since I couldn't shake the image of my father, descended from Native Americans, hiding from me that he carried in his DNA the sum total of all Western music from the last century and every century to come. I felt less and less enlightened, more and more bitter.

So, one night, I desperately decided to do what seemed like the only way not to go completely senile: at the end of a concert at The Great American Music Hall, under the gilded decorations, I offered to buy a drink for a young, easy-going girl who was the same age as my daughter, and my fiancée in 1984: she'd reminded me of both of them, unfortunately. The last year had taken its toll on me: my face was gaunt, my eyes sagged; and my mouth looked like a vampire's. But with a nice suede jacket, the right shoes and collar to go with it, it all worked for a girl who was looking for a fatherly figure in the darkness.

We made love at her parents' house since they were out, and when I saw that her mother had a used Martin, I played a little something to help her fall asleep. At first, it was hard, because the nine measures forced their way out through my fingers like Eve from Adam's rib. 'Oh, I like that. It's nice. Play it again, please,' she said, before mumbling: 'that's your style.'

And as she closed her eyes, it became obvious: this piece had never been played before. It was from the future, and the reason I didn't recognise it was because I couldn't have ever heard it before.

I laughed, without waking her up. Then I went out onto the landing for a smoke, and beneath the stars I felt like I was 20 years old again. Finally, I understood the way destiny worked: 'Walking Backwards' wasn't fated for me, had never been, and it had become my song by accident, after some kind of happenstance, short-circuited by my father and all these Native Americans; the piece that was meant for me, and that didn't exist yet, was this one. It was for me, had been waiting for me, and all I had to do was take it, create it, make it big!

At long last...

F

¶ But the next day, at the studio, I began to doubt myself more and more. I'd sobered up. The girl had been pretty, but I probably wouldn't ever see her again. Maybe those nine measures were from a very distant future, maybe they weren't meant to be mine. After all, the Sélène cylinders had been engraved with music from around the world to the end of all time. What reason did I have to think that this piece was the music of tomorrow, rather than the next century? I sat on the stool with the Gibson in my hand, and couldn't express the music the way I'd hoped to. I was frustrated, and everything sounded forced. Of course I could just imitate the notes, play the sequence straight through, but I wasn't sure anymore that I had the power to make that music simply be, the way I'd thought I could the night before. I forced myself to reproduce it on a Korg, then let the song burst out, by broadening the range and sounds; it was almost there, but not quite, like a balled-up sheet of paper I couldn't quite smooth out completely, which kept crinkling despite my efforts to open it up fully, or like a door that I'd thought was wide open at a distance, but which, I realised when I approached its threshold, perhaps because I'd underestimated how tall I actually was or how much I actually weighed, I would not be able to enter.

I used multi-effect pedals and tried everything. Then I asked Joey to help me break down the amps, take apart the connections, and reassemble the circuits. I was trying to reach for the sound of tomorrow, in the hope that it might be mine.

In vain.

I was pissed off, I blamed Joey – who slammed the door shut.

In the end, I simply had no way to play those nine measures; they never sounded the way they were supposed to. I went into a black rage, wrecked half the stuff in the room, and I'm almost certain I set fire to the apartment.

Well, I don't remember any of this clearly, of course, because that night I ended up at San Francisco General Hospital, where Joey, my singer, and Wave Packet's manager found me the next day. I only had superficial wounds, but I'd escaped safely. 'You're a survivor!' my old friend the singer wailed into my arms. And I realised that I'd been an unworthy friend. I started crying, called myself an idiot, and promised the whole group that we were going to record this damn album all together.

¶ In the fire, the trunk, the three cylinders, the phonograph, and my papers had all gone up in smoke.

VIII.

Now I just wanted to find the truth of new songs within myself, and not in repeating the past; it was time to express what belonged to me, and me alone.

During the first recording sessions, I could feel all the memories of the year that had just gone by falling away from me: Jean–Luc Massenet; his uncle; Constantin Sélène, soldier of the empire; the monk Fernando Paiva; the Native Americans of the Bay. They all went quiet in my head, and I faintly remembered, beyond the last reverberations of my madness, the simple feeling of that girl, that night with her, and that moment in my life that had spoken to me alone. For the first time in many years, I felt renewed and inspired. Joey was working in other studios, where I came to set up guitars for the song. I only had one song, but the entire album would come out of it.

After it was finished, both of the guys behind the glass started drinking beers. We could hear them in the empty studios. Joey pointed me towards what was still missing: 'This is solid work, but it's like a sleeping body you can't be bothered to give a bit of fucking love to. Know what I'm saying? Listen to the chorus...' I wasn't annoyed at all, and I encouraged Joey to give me a few suggestions. 'Switch the chord progression, and bring that little phrase in and out, OK? Let's do it!' He sang it softly: 'One, two, three... seven, eight, nine measures. And that's it!' I smiled. Through him, I'd found the missing condition. I'd managed to lose and somehow find again what was needed to make it appear.

'You're right.' In a single take, I recorded the phrase and the song was transformed.

'Whoa... I think you've got something epic here. It's something I've never heard before...' Even if Joey was drunk, I was happy to believe him, even just a little. 'Fuck, this is going to be better than "Walking Backwards"!' His eyes were moist. 'You're going to be remembered for this, my man.' I decided to give the song a French title, 'Les Rouleaux de bois', and Joey would get some credit for it.

For the first time in years and years, I slept happily, without any thoughts in my mind.

❡ Early in the morning, my daughter called. She was just back from South Korea; I'd actually forgotten about her.

She introduced me to her boyfriend, and I made them some coffee. Jin was a student, a music lover, and my daughter had told him about me. He definitely knew about 'Walking Backwards'. When he asked me how I wrote it, I pretended to remember and I smiled: it was time to tell the story once again.

My girl knew her father's tried–and–true ramblings by heart, so she flipped through a celebrity magazine and let us talk in the kitchen. Jin was fun to talk to, as curious as an eighties kid from the American indie scene, and even as I could see how he saw me as an ambassador from an era that seemed just as far away to him as World War Two, I knew I had the future with me: 'Les Rouleaux de bois'. It occurred to me to play him the demo from the day before, but I held back from this smug idea, and I asked him about the rise of Asia's music scene.

'I think everything's happening over there, sir,' he answered.

F

That was when he pulled an iPod out of his sweatshirt: he pressed his thumb on the scrolling menu and gave me the headphones.

'What's this?'

An unease rose in my gut, and I could feel sweat beading on my forehead. This wasn't just a premonition. He told me the name of the band. For six months, obsessed as I'd been with the wooden cylinders, I hadn't kept up with the news. Apparently all the young kids wanted to sound like this band.

'Say that again?'

He smiled slowly and tiny crinkles appeared around his eyelids as he told me: 'I'd have thought you would already know about this. It's all anybody talks about. This bit is incredible. It's *the music of the future.*'

My face was pale and my hands were shaking as I plugged the headphones into my ears. He flicked his finger over the screen to show me the lyrics of the song in Korean.

As soon as I heard the first measure, I recognised it.

EILEEN QUINLAN

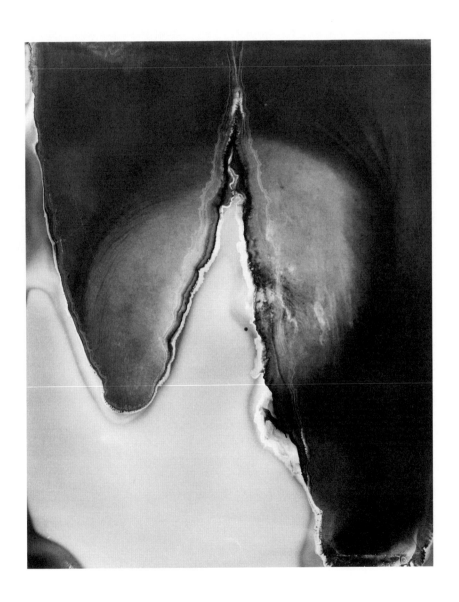

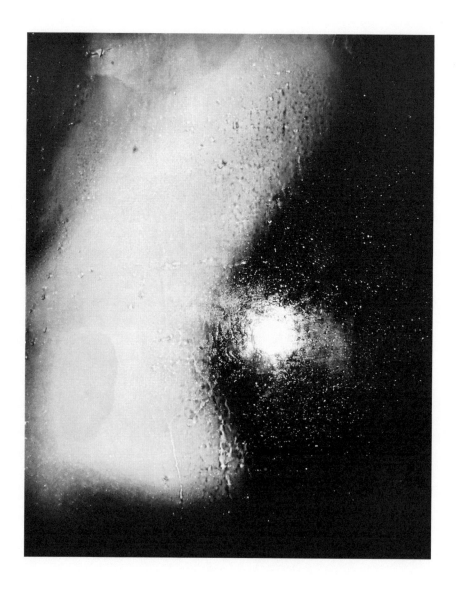

XIII

BASIC NEEDS

BY

EVAN HARRIS

I KNOW THE DATE the bankers visited the children because I recorded it in an email to a friend. It was 3 December 2012, two months after I'd started working at the primary school in Leytonstone; three before I'd quit. During the previous summer I'd exhausted my overdraft and stamina for job application forms. Like many young graduates, I took work as a teaching assistant through a temp agency because it required no experience and there were positions available.[1]

Miss E. had prepared the class, pitching her voice above the clatter and shriek of thirty children clearing their desks.

'Some very important people are generously giving you their time,' she said. 'I'm expecting your best behaviour.'

She aimed her finger at my primary charge, Faaruq.

'I don't want a squeak out of you,' she said. 'Sir will be watching you like a hawk, won't you sir?'

I raised my eyebrows, as if in assent.

The group from Barclays bank examined the colourful wall displays, their hands folded across their chests or holstered in their smart-casual pockets.[2] One politely asked if I could make for the children sufficient copies of the worksheet they had brought to structure their informal lesson. They had come to impart financial prudence to the children, community outreach as part of the bank's 'corporate citizenship' programme, and seemed enamoured with the children's volubility, if at first a little awkward managing it. As they fielded questions from the students about their careers and the banking system, the bankers exchanged with each other the kind of glances you give to close friends to discreetly communicate surprise, shock or pleasure. I imagined them later returning home on the tube, resting their heads on the window-glass, eyes narrowed as they contemplated their encounter in the school, and later reporting to the community outreach coordinator that they had learned as much from the experience as the children had.

In class, the most loaded glance between the bankers came when the confidently smart but contrary child Duane, illicitly pivoting on the hind legs of his chair, raised

---

[1] I earned £290 net a week. The temp agency took a cut and employed what is called an umbrella company to administer their payroll to temps, through which you hold travel and food costs against income tax – again for a service fee. Using this company was non-negotiable. That is, the state paid me to work in a state school, and two private companies took a cut of my wages – and one of these companies was employed so that I wouldn't pay any tax back to the state. Temps are not entitled to holiday pay; there are eleven weeks of mandatory holiday in the school year.

[2] Between 2000 and 2011 Barclays' tax avoidance division generated £9.5bn in revenue. A member of the parliamentary commission on banking standards accused the bank of 'industrial scale tax avoidance'.

a hand for permission to speak. 'Is the banks a safe place to put our money, then? My Dad says there was a crash or something. Says it's like gambling.'

Miss E. winced and gave him her own glance, but smiles appeared in series across the bankers' faces. One leaned forward on his child-sized chair and said, 'There are lots of rules now. The government gives you a kind of promise. Perfectly safe.'

A quick exit poll of the children as they sped out of the classroom for break suggested not all had been impressed by the prospect of a career in finance. Some, clutching their coats under their arms and trying to shake me off, said yes they would like to be a banker when they grow up because they make lots of money and are powerful. Faaruq asked if the bankers made enough money to buy iPhones. I told them that they did and more, and he was sold. Others were unchanged: their aim, they said, remained to be a footballer or a pop star like Rihanna. To a greater or lesser extent, regardless of the professions to which the children aspired, inherent to their aspirations was the accumulation of material wealth. When I was 9, I wanted to be a marine biologist, as a teenager, a musician, though I sometimes enjoyed the fantasy of wearing a suit to a steel and glass office and being very, very rich. Each of my youthful projections assumed what I now understand to be an above average disposable income, and I presume that I am not unusual in this regard.[3] The thought embarrasses me now, but sometimes I imagined being invited back to my school to impart my wisdom to the children, though mainly to flaunt my wealth in the faces of teachers who said I would amount to very little, the way I was going. And here I was, back in the classroom.

❡ I first drafted this essay from a different class, sixteen months hence: I was awarded a scholarship to study creative writing in the US, for which applications I composed a short story based on my experiences at the school. It adhered pretty closely to real events, though it didn't occur to me to include the visit from the bankers. In a fiction it would have seemed implausible, I think now, a facile allegory that attributed to the bankers the greatest responsibility for the limitations of the children's lives, obscuring with a popular bogey(wo)man the systemic inequities of the school and elsewhere.

The story did not succeed: in changed circumstances the sublimation of past labour was painful, and fiction seemed inadequate to the complexity of experience and the imperative to record it. Unable to evade the consequence of the work, I later wrote this essay of recensions to exhibit and recontextualise my relationships to three children as staged in the story. The intention was to examine at one remove both my

---

[3.] In 2014, UK median income for full-time employees was £27,195. Newly qualified teachers begin around £22,000, but with her experience Miss E. would be nearer £30,000. If you are fortunate enough to be a contracted teaching assistant you might get £17,000; if you're not contracted it's more like £12,000.

wage labour and the process of literary composition to better understand my discom-
fort with both.

I.

*In class, David sits between Tayden and Faaruq at the 'Air Table'. Tables are named after
Presocratic elements; Miss E. has named this one for its low academic ability. David is
a buffer between the boys, two sincere 9-year-olds who, Miss E. insists, would kill each
other if left unattended. David doubts this prediction. Mostly, Tayden is placid, mouth
agape, perfect teeth displayed like an advert for toothpaste, a substance often encrusted at
the corners of his lips. His thoughts and sensations seem dulled by a fog, and David often
wonders if he is sedated.*

*Sedation is what Miss E. wishes for Faaruq; she sometimes suggests, in jest, that
they spike his water bottle. The boy is an elastic-limbed fidget, excited by everything in the
class but the work. Pencils are his favourite, but anything to hand will do. Except when sad,
Faaruq overflows with energy and David takes the shocks. It displeases him, but it pays
his rent and distracts him from his sadness the way a stubbed toe momentarily obscures
toothache.*

¶ Both boys had arrived to the UK as very young children, though neither could
recall for me anything of their countries of birth (the Democratic Republic of Congo
and Somalia). Their recall was limited to mobile phones, videogames, football.
Occasionally the boys would do some work and seek my praise for it; occasionally
my praise delighted them. When, for example, examining Faaruq's work I would af-
firm that he had grasped, at least for the last thirty minutes (he would not remember it
the next day), the mathematical concept of long division, he would perform the same
bombastic jig with which he celebrated his football goals at break time. Then Miss E.,
hands planted on hips – sometimes offering me a comradely glance or wink – would
shout at Faaruq for being silly and disruptive.

I was well-behaved in primary school. I remember the force of the teacher's
raised voice and emphatic gestures, but I don't recall fearing them; they weren't for
good boys like me. I remember watching in horror as Jeremy, one of the kids in Mr
James's class, shrugged off such force, and Mr James with Jeremy's collar bunched in
his fist howling and sneering insults in Jeremy's face. It's improbable that I can recall
it with such clarity, but, visualising it now, Mr James's face is puce and Jeremy's the
kind of ill red you get with dangerous fever or a tantrum protracted to the point of
exhaustion. Mr James was my favourite teacher. Watching him intimidate Jeremy I
experienced a kind of thrilled awe at the intransigence of adult justice. I knew what
to do, it made me feel safe. I was a good kid and Jeremy was bad, that's what everyone
was told, that's what I believed and was rewarded for.

E

Every day, watching small children get similarly shamed and intimidated by teachers, memories like this reemerged, and I watched with detached impotence, this time invested with that power to administer adult justice to children but not to other adults, my material needs dependent on a closed system that valourised this kind of punishment. I was overwhelmed with my own shame until I learned to distract myself by counting my wage in hourly increments until it reached the figure of my weekly rent.

In my experience of working in schools, unless they had a particular enthusiasm for it, teaching assistants enjoyed the privilege of diminished responsibility for classroom order. That is, though I was expected to support the teacher's system of discipline, the responsibility ultimately lay with the teacher – I could just attend to the small group I had been assigned.[4] Though I did resort to threats, and raised my voice, I tried to be patient and take the children's interests seriously, spoke to them as if they were adults, and politely took interest in their enthusiasm for football or phones. Faaruq had a basic model Blackberry. He told me he was going to upgrade soon; his dad was always going to take him to the phone shop at the weekend to arrange it. He pestered me for weeks to see what phone I had, and I deferred: the school had a 'no phones in class' policy, which I didn't want to embarrass myself by breaking, and the boys were likely to be agitated by me showing it. One day I bargained with them a look at my phone for half a page of geometry, and pulled from my pocket the scuffed basic smartphone and laid it on the table. I don't think he could help it, the way you can't because you're uninhibited and having fun.

'That's a shit phone, sir, that is.'

Faaruq clamped his hands to his mouth as if he were a cartoon character in error, given added effect by eyes that anyway naturally protruded. You can sense it bodily when someone is genuinely frightened; if you spend enough time with kids you know the difference between the act and the real thing. Faaruq was genuinely frightened. 9 years old, he had sworn at a teacher. I thought he was wonderful; Miss E. gave him a verbal hammering worthy of Mr James. As encouragement to improve himself, at high volume to Faaruq's face she told him he was a failure, a lost cause. He was sent

---

[4] I had briefly worked at another school with a similar demographic intake as the one in Leytonstone. It had a policy of less threatening discipline that used a complex system of charts the children were expected to administer themselves – the children policing and shaming each other. The teachers were discouraged from raising their voices and rarely did. Its more insidious method still disturbed me, but it at least created a more pleasant atmosphere, and in it children of all abilities seemed more productive. I remember being awed that a 9-year-old was reading DAVID COPPERFIELD of his own volition and could tell me all about it. I wanted to tell him that Dickens had become a common reference again for conditions in contemporary London.

to the head teacher for more of the same, and a letter followed him home that evening. They made him deliver me a spoken and written apology the next day. I could sense that it was genuine.

¶ Tayden and Faaruq had a thing for pencils. They took pencils from students, from the table's central stationery container, they took pencils from each other. They took pencils surreptitiously and they snatched. They put pencils in their pockets, on their laps, kept pencils under their bums like hens do eggs. When told to stand and move their laminated name tag to the red zone of the discipline wall chart, I would hear turn across the textured plastic of the standardised school chair the wood–timbre patter of hexagonal pencils. With a little force a sharp nib punctures easily the soft epidermis of a child's too–slow hand. The boys used pencils in play and in anger.

This boy, Faaruq, is at the end of a row of children, as far from Miss E. as he can sit. In his lap he has a collection of yellow–and–black striped pencils, the domed red ends woody with tooth–chew. He takes one of the pencils, pointed nib facing out, and slowly raises it to the neck of the girl that sits before him. His eyes are wide, his mouth an O of anticipation. David watches Faaruq inch the pencil forward. The school operates a colour–coded warning system. Faaruq is already on yellow. If David intervenes, Miss E. will move Faaruq to red. If Faaruq is on red at the day's end, he will be sent to the deputy headmaster, who will ask Faaruq's parents to enact retribution. It is true that every time this justice is performed Faaruq is much quieter, much better behaved the next day; his eyes are unfocused, his rest- less energy is absent; each time an adult addresses him, he flinches against his chair.

What can David do? However he acts, the result will be the same. If he reprimands Faaruq, Miss E. will move his name to red. If he does nothing, then the girl in front of Faaruq will feel the point of a pencil in her neck, will cry out to Miss E., who will then reprimand Faaruq and move his name to red. And this, of course, is what happens: Faaruq's name is again a red name, again he is a bad boy.

¶ In the story, the pencil serves as a continuous metaphor for violence – the way structural violence (systemic, impersonal) is resisted or protested with direct physical violence. A pencil sharpened by David and given to Faaruq as an instrument to write with is used instead as a dangerous prop in a play of resistance. The fiction climaxes when Faaruq is excluded from mainstream education for stabbing Tayden with a pen- cil. In reality, Faaruq did get Tayden in the hand. He wasn't excluded but the word was increasingly used in teachers' repertoires of threats, along with predictions of a dismal future.

Miss E. had two sons, and I think it's fair to say she was a proud mother – proud both of her sons and her maternal practice. To emphasise the qualitative difference in parental care between that which her sons received and that which, say, Faaruq received, she would boast about the limits she set on her sons' gaming time and how high her sons' reading levels were. Nearing Christmas, she took me aside and described for me the difference between the resources allocated for the Christmas play in this school compared to that in her sons'. 'They have theatre lights,' she said. 'They've been rehearsing for two months already.'

Miss E. lived in Archway but sent her boys to school in Highgate; had moved to the former so that she would be in the catchment area of the latter, where it's unlikely she would have been able to afford a property on her teacher's salary. Like some of her colleagues, she was critical of the Leytonstone school's management, but attributed most of its difficulties to the children and their families, without acknowledging, to me at least, that the children's families didn't have the resources for the kind of aspirational move she had achieved. Instead, Miss E. contrasted her students' and her sons' differences in privilege in meritocratic and moral measures – that is, by the organising reason of the classroom.

So that my treatment of the children would be well-informed, she sometimes took me aside to narrate their backgrounds: incarcerated siblings, absent fathers, benefit claimants, and so on. She would reel off in disgust how many kids by how many fathers an unemployed single mother had, childcare administered by plasma widescreen. This attitude, that students' social and academic limits are set before they enter school, and that a student's deviation from school norms is a confirmation of delinquency as opposed to an expression of need, was shared by many of the staff of the five schools I worked in over a year. This cynicism affirms and reinscribes a fact of predetermined lives: depending on the analysis, UK social mobility since 1970 has been either static or in decline. That means there is a diminished possibility that these children will ever earn more than their parents do. Their parents don't earn much. There are 326 administrative boroughs in England; this school is in Waltham Forest, which is the fifteenth most deprived. That's determined by the measurement of seven domains: income deprivation; employment deprivation; health deprivation and disability; education, skills and training deprivation; barriers to housing and services; living environment deprivation; crime. The usual metric for students' poverty in a school is their entitlement to free school meals; in this school almost half were entitled, more than double the borough average. Faaruq and Tayden were entitled. In as blasé a tone as if only predicting their maths grades, Miss E. had marked the pair out for unemployment or prison. Both boys were enthusiastic about violent games like CALL OF DUTY and FAR CRY; they told me they aspired to become soldiers.

II.

For a month David has been phone-checking for messages when the girl takes his hand in the school yard. She leads him away from the fence he leans on. Beneath one of the school's silver birches she pauses to speak.

Her language is unfamiliar. David grasps at the sounds to stitch them into sentences but they shape-shift and vanish like smoke. She's pointing somewhere and he looks and it makes no sense. A cacophony whirls and howls around them, the enormous aggregate of four hundred voices, four hundred children with half an hour to play. The girl frowns below the elasticated hem of her black hijab. He balls his hands and blows on them. The girl takes his hands and exaggeratedly puffs, her cheeks inflated and her lips pushed out. She squeals, delighted by the coils of clouded vapour and the rude noises that ripple from her lips. He smiles: for a moment she has distracted him. The bell rings. Break time is over.

❡ Hani was 8; she spoke no English. Three months earlier she had arrived in London from Gambia, and she had two favourite games. One was sneaking from the rear of and onto the bench I sat alone on, leaping onto my back, and clamping herself to my body with surprisingly powerful limbs as I applied evasive manoeuvres and tried to peel her off. The other was pulling me up from my seat, and, palms against my belly, pushing me backward until I collided with a tree or post or the fence that delineated the school football pitch's perimeter. I would see through my eyelashes her dental arcs in a mouth agape with anticipation. As I struck a solid upright she stamped around in comic delight while I feigned confusion and shock.

In the fiction Hani is a kind of platonic substitute for David's ex-lover. They keep each other company at break time and get pleasure from play. She is an opportunity for David to invest his care in someone receptive to it; he sees the investigation of Hani's life as an opportunity for redeeming his disintegrated relationship. He imagines telling his ex a narrative composed of African stereotype and cliché.

David has solved the mystery, he is a stream of sympathetic knowledge. Gambian scrubland, relatives executed in the doorways of their homes, a brave family in the back of a lurching truck. He has taught her English and she is making friends at school, but she always comes to visit him on the bench. She is complex: though she is wide-eyed excitement itself, she has frequent moments of contemplation, insights that only early trauma can nurture. He knows she will grow to be a sophisticated and socially conscious adult, a human rights activist or community leader.

And the teacher's privilege: knowing that in some way he contributed to her success.

❡ I knew nothing of Hani's life, couldn't have. Neither she nor her parents spoke English and I only managed to teach her a few English nouns at break time; understandably she just wanted to play. She was not unusual: in the school, the number of children whose first language was not English was well above the national average;

thirty-eight different languages were spoken in total. The number of children who were learning English from scratch was also well above average, and there were very few additional resources provided for them – they had to participate in lessons with the fluently communicating children.[5] Hani once led me by the hand into her classroom to show me her workbook – it contained simple drawings and addition, nothing tailored to an English learner.

My and David's motivations for investigating Hani's background were different, or I withheld from the fiction a congruity that would necessitate greater exploration of character. I did not imagine the articulation of Hani's story as leverage in a relationship, but perhaps I could have imagined it as a kind of intellectual currency to spend amongst my politically concerned friends, redeeming the drudgery with a little exotic trivia; on reflection, comparable to the way I imagined the bankers would circulate in conversation their own edifying experiences with the children. Today I learned something, at least. Yet while it provided the fiction with a little plot, it was in reality appealing to learn about Hani's life – I fleetingly pretended that the information I found would improve her school experience. But most of all it alleviated the boredom.

My investigations yielded very little. When I asked her teacher what language Hani spoke, so that I could use Google Translate to teach her nouns, the teacher suggested Gambian. There is no Gambian language: the country is composed of many ethnic groups, each with its own language or dialect. The official state language is English.

David sits on the bench, and she wriggles her body onto his lap. He slides her off onto the bench, beside him. Look, he says, pointing at his phone, Gambia. She pulls his hand and smears hers across the screen. Gambia, she says. Wait, he says, look. He zooms in on the list of languages, speaks each name in turn: Mandinka, Fula, Wolof, Serer, Jola, Serahule. Hani says: Serahule! David points at Hani. Serahule, he says. Serahule! she repeats. He sees that Serahule make only 9 per cent of the population. Why has her family come here? Hani grasps the phone again, presses a button, takes a photo of David's knees. She laughs, climbs onto the bench, smothers his back and squeals with delight.

❡ Depending on the source, female genital mutilation (FGM) is widespread or universal in Serahule culture, and is not uncommon in the UK: an estimated 137,000 girls have had it done to them in this country, with another 24,000 at risk annually.

---

[5] The headteacher purchased for the school thirty iPads and a charging station the size of a family refrigerator. Under supervision, the children could use the iPads once a week to do the same basic IT work they used to do on PCs. The staff agreed that this wasn't the most appropriate use of a very limited school budget.

I deployed this in the fiction as an extreme test of David's passivity, introduced through a character who can easily seem constructed to give the fiction weight: an energetic smiling young girl who cannot communicate, who can neither confirm nor reject David's assumption of abuse.

My assumption. When I raised it in the staffroom at lunchtime, a veteran and contracted teaching assistant casually added that there were lots of girls entering the nursery who had had it done, and 'it's a mess when you take them to the loo'. The other staff nodded in acknowledgment or tutted, returned to their phones, spooning into their mouths reheated leftovers from Tupperware containers.

In the fiction, David tentatively goes to broach the issue with the head teacher and finds Faaruq crying on the carpet outside her office. The head teacher impatiently – her own lunch has been disrupted – tells Faaruq that she doesn't want boys like him in the school, and asks David to agree. David doesn't mention FGM. I didn't even go to her office.

In 2014, the year after I worked in the school, following an advocacy campaign by NGOs and the *GUARDIAN*, the Minister for Education wrote to schools to remind them of their responsibilities to girls regarding FGM, and the government announced programmes and guidelines to prevent its occurrence. I do not know to what extent they have been implemented. I do know Hani's teacher never determined what language she spoke.

Hani and I interacted less and less in the five months I worked at the school. I tired of the repetition of push and clamber and my inability to interpret anything from her speech; Hani seemed dejected by my diminished enthusiasm for imaginative play. She sometimes found company in other social outliers and mimicked the dance routines they performed behind the football goal. Sometimes she walked the perimeter fence alone.

III.

As part of his daily routine, David hunches on a child's chair, sharpening pencils after class. One hundred pencils; 3.3 pencils per child in class 5D. His phone is on the table; he reads news articles as he works wood. Also it's near in case it should ring. Turning hands carve away the seconds, he hears them fall from the clock. He tries to calculate how many hours, how much total carved from how much total life. He strokes his phone screen. The classroom is empty. Outside it's dusk but in class it's clinically bright.

¶ The headmistress didn't want me to leave the job. I was a good worker, she said, and I had a rapport with the children. I sold all my saleable possessions except my MacBook and phone and moved to Budapest, because there were jobs available with sufficient disparity between income and rent that I could save a thousand dollars for graduate school applications. I wrote the story in the afternoon breaks of thirteen-hour workdays teaching call centre managers, accountants and IT workers who administered the trunk systems of banks. They were learning English to better their career prospects; some wanted to move to London. I applied to ten funded creative writing programmes and was accepted at the only one I did not send this story to.

❡ The group from Barclays were here to deliver the children a short informal lesson about managing personal finances. They asked the children rowed on the carpet to raise their hands to suggest things that they, the children, needed in their lives. We got clothes, food, phones, Playstation, books, cinema trips, ice-skating (some with their parents had visited the Winter Wonderland rink in West London). The bankers then asked the children to suggest a country that isn't as rich as England. Someone suggested Africa; the bankers exchanged one of those impressed glances and used Africa as their example.[6]

'So, do people in Africa need the same things as you or different?'

'Different!'

'OK. Great. Wow. Well, what do they need then?'

The children wobbled on their knees or bums, waving arms in the air — some supported with a hand the bicep of the waving arm as if they might raise it higher, off their shoulder.

'Water!'

'Good.'

'Oooh, oooh, I know! Food!'

'Excellent.'

The bankers continued to elicit suggestions until they had filled the whiteboard with basic needs. They used a triangle to illustrate that personal finances should be arranged by a hierarchy of needs, with these basic needs in the lowest stratum of the hierarchy. The takeaway message was: when you have money you take care of these needs first. When the children were split into groups to negotiate priorities amongst themselves using a hypothetical monthly budget, a triangle diagram and symbols that represented needs and responsibilities, I had a hard time convincing Faaruq and Tayden to prioritise the gas bill over a new videogame.

'What about heating when it's cold in the winter?'

'Put my coat on!'

'But your hands will be too cold to use the controller.'

[6.] About a third of the class were either born in Africa or their family was born in Africa, which is, famously, a continent not a country. A financial manager's average base salary is £52,000/year before bonuses and such.

'Sir, I've got gloves!'

¶ At the end of the session, the bankers distributed to the children blue HB pencils bearing an embossed Barclays logo. They told the kids to work hard, dream hard, and waved as they departed to give their presentation and branded stationery to Miss M.'s class, next door.

5D were unusually animated. They excitedly exchanged facts they had retained from the talk; some waved aloft their Barclays pencils as if they were enchanted wands and struck each other with extemporised curses. Miss E. yelled at them to calm down. They would never be bankers, she said and gave me a glance, if they didn't behave themselves. Faaruq effervesced amongst the standardised furniture, his eyes more cartoonish than usual. He tracked and disappeared the unattended pencils, pursing his lips the way some kids do when they think they're getting away with it. To distract him from imminent punishment, I asked if he would like to be a banker. He asked if they made enough money to buy iPhones; I told him they did and more. I made my disappointed face and shook my head to deter him from his next victim. Tayden glazedly looked out of the window, his lips as always glossy and unlatched. He clutched tight to his chest the unexpected pencil – then squirmed away from Faaruq's creeping hand.

INTERVIEW

CALLY SPOONER

TOWARDS THE END of our conversation at her studio above Ridley Road, a busy street market in Hackney East London, Cally Spooner tells me she's been reading a lot of Kathy Acker. Spooner is an artist whose output includes essays and novels, radio broadcasts, film installations, plays and a musical. Her work often pulls together forms of speech and movement associated with the kinds of situations in which bodies are under pressure to perform and affect each other – the workplace, the sports field, the stage. Like Acker's writing, Spooner's work is not entirely outsourced but she often appropriates from other sources, from comments sections to meeting notes from an advertising agency. In 'Against Ordinary Language: The Language of the Body', which first appeared in the anthology THE LAST SEX: FEMINISM AND OUTLAW BODIES (1993), Acker writes about breaking down your muscles while bodybuilding so they grow back larger than before – this kind of building is 'working around failure'. The language that belongs in the gym is repetitive, and can be harnessed to meet that which 'cannot be fully controlled and known': the body. 'I feel like I've been thinking about a lot of the same things as her but doing it in an entirely different way,' says Spooner. 'It's like I got it completely the wrong way round.'

Spooner's studio is a long and thin office space with some storage at one end. She has shared the space with another artist since she recently came to terms with the fact that she doesn't have a studio practice – she has been working in public. She goes to Ridley Road to read books and send emails. A series of musical performances staged across Europe – Berlin, London – under the title AND YOU WERE WONDERFUL, ON STAGE (2013-2015) recently culminated in a five-screen film installation at the Stedelijk Museum, Amsterdam. It's a complex musical performance by singers, dancers and a film crew that appears to continually assemble and disassemble itself at the same time as it reproduces itself. A new work for six dancers based on corporate techniques to produce conflict and intimacy as affect in working environments, titled ON FALSE TEARS AND OUTSOURCING, will be on view at the New Museum, New York from April 2016.

A reader of theory as well as fiction and poetry, Spooner cites texts by Michel Foucault, Umberto Eco, and the sociologist and theorist of 'immaterial labour' Maurizio Lazzarato. These texts are, she tells me, understood through real-world encounters and experiences, from living with an air-con unit on residency in Texas, to working in advertising and obsessing about a section of Frank O'Hara's 'Having a Coke with You':

> I look
> at you and I would rather look at you than all the portraits in the world
> except possibly for the Polish Rider occasionally and anyway it's in the Frick
> which thank heavens you haven't gone to yet so we can go together the first time

Spooner seems to be continually breaking everything down in order to expose the conditions in which people and things make and transfer meaning, in the hope that she will one day be able to write *through* these mechanics, rather than *about* them. She is breaking it all down in order to get stronger, you might say, using the voices of others to find her own.

Q. THE WHITE REVIEW — You made the choreography for your show at the New Museum during your show at Vleeshal [both titled ON FALSE TEARS AND OUTSOURCING]. What can visitors to your New York show expect to see, and how did you develop the piece?

A. CALLY SPOONER — It's a piece for six dancers. At the New Museum, the architectural lights will be multiplied – the whole ceiling is going to be full of them – so their bodies will be extremely visible. The piece is structured through this meeting technique called 'stand up scrum', in which you have to ask each other: 'What did you do yesterday?' 'What will you do today?' 'What obstacles stand in your way?' It's a technique I was managed with at the advertising agency where I used to work, and where I wrote the musical (AND YOU WERE WONDERFUL, ON STAGE). It's a way of solving problems really fast, putting intimacy in a group, and getting people to self-organise so they don't require an external manager. It's about producing aggression.

Q. THE WHITE REVIEW — About creating confrontation?

A. CALLY SPOONER — Exactly. Get fired up. Build a team. Be intimate. Disclose: 'This didn't work, you didn't work, you failed, I failed…' It's a useful model to think about intimacy and teamwork in an engineered situation. You have to produce these affects at 9 a.m. in order to work. You have to remain intimately bound to one another whilst being violently and competitively separate.

The piece was workshopped with a film director and a rugby coach. The dancers were trained in onscreen affect and competitive contact sport moves, and then instructed to self-organise. They were given a number of different simple tasks driven by this one contradictory choreographic instruction – to

remain proximate and separate. They'll be very close and then they'll take out each other's knees and tackle each other, or they have to get up off the floor but only using the other person's face. So they move from gestures of extreme closeness to using them as physical support to complete the task.

I used to have those meetings in a glass meeting room, so I'm thinking a lot about Dan Graham and corporate space, and trying to use the institution and its architectures as parameters, as a readymade, without being cynical – it's not a work that doesn't need an artist. They'll be performing this piece all day in the space downstairs in the lobby, which has a glass wall.

Q. THE WHITE REVIEW — And that glass wall divides the gallery from a café space, right?

A. CALLY SPOONER — Yeah, it's wild. These bodies will be in there all the time fighting and embracing. Bodies up against the glass…

Q. THE WHITE REVIEW — So you'll be able to choose whether to view the gallery as a stage, from the outside, or the inside?

A. CALLY SPOONER — Yeah! It's a contradictory choreographic instruction that plays itself out all day every day and people watch, either in very close fleshy proximity or behind this glass screen. On the other side of the glass you're safe. We see conflict playing itself out all the time through screens but we also carry it with us every day. I made a piece while I was on residency in Texas last autumn where I multiplied the lights to create a very bright daylight condition in the room and I turned the temperature up to body temperature. You had to deal with it. Your body responded.

Q. THE WHITE REVIEW — Presumably in Texas everyone is used to air-conditioned spaces?

A. CALLY SPOONER —— Well that's what got me thinking about it. The whole time I was there I was air-conditioned. I had the machine that powered the whole building's air con right outside my apartment. It was so aggressive – my whole room would vibrate! Air conditioning is so weird, right? Everybody is the same temperature and everyone's experiencing the exact same air condition in every part of the building. It helps people work better. It's an architecture that's supposed to neutralise everything, but it has this dirty great engine behind it. It was 36 degrees outside in Texas. I'd never been to a part of the world where I had to be neutralised like that. I was reading THE OPEN WORK by Eco, the section 'Form As a Social Commitment'. He talks about the moment when you become completely alienated by your own production because it's too smooth-functioning – your tools are no longer irksome. Eco is calling for irksome tools, or an awareness of the apparatus and its filthiness, because once you have to grapple with that apparatus you're not alienated from your own production any more.

I'm really obsessed with things like Xenomania [a British songwriting and production team founded by Brian Higgins] where you have musicians in the attic producing surf guitar riffs, or someone downstairs producing rhythms on drums all day, and the producers come along and stitch a song together. It's really administrative and unromantic but it produces music that has this crazy impact on people. I think a lot about how you can just administrate affect. For the last three weeks at Vleeshal I used the space as a kind of pop production factory. I was instructing in-house musicians via email to produce emotional songs. We made this pop song, which in the end wasn't very...

Q. THE WHITE REVIEW —— Emotive?

A. CALLY SPOONER —— Exactly! It was actually really funny. I also set up a Stanislavski training course to train financiers to produce tears. There's a lot of group work. You learn to identify things that are upsetting, things that are external to you, and how to treat those emotions as objects that you can handle and use, rather than letting them demolish you.

In SIGNS AND MACHINES: CAPITALISM AND THE PRODUCTION OF SUBJECTIVITY, Maurizio Lazzarato talks about this idea of the performative, which arises from meshing the fleshy humanism of self-realisation with the hardcore mechanic processes used to assess performance and manage bodies and outputs, such as key performances indictors diagrams, data... The human becomes a terminal for these things. He speaks of a form of life that is 'other' to the performative; a space that has liveliness in it, which is to do with risk and emotion and publicness. He called that an aesthetic space, but of course that which is aesthetic, affecting and lively could be as manufactured and managed as the performative, which he deems so subjugating. I'm still trying to work out what this aesthetic space is exactly. I was thinking about the manufacturing of affect and the Stanislavski method, how you can literally train to produce affect, by bringing your personal space to work. I felt, naively, from a distance without knowing anything about The Method, that this was fucked up. So then I brought The Method to my show and set these training sessions up. There was a lot of imagining oranges and singing to your coat as if it was your grandma, but that diminishes what it was. I can cry if I return to this particular place because it evokes these very personal instances. But then I had to train too. The trainer, Arnica Elsendoorn, said it was very bad if I didn't.

Q. THE WHITE REVIEW — How did the fact that you had to participate in the course, rather than just outsource the work to a trained professional as you had planned, change the work you intended to make?

A. CALLY SPOONER — What really got me was that I just felt awful about my work. I was like, what am I doing? It made me sad that I couldn't, as an artist, speak of that which was positive, that which actually makes me incredibly happy, or strong – I was too busy making financiers cry or talking about how subjected I am by particular forms of life and language. Somehow in my repertoire of utterance there had been no room to plainly celebrate the fact that there was this thing that I considered really joyful. That was when I cried. I was thinking about Frank O'Hara's 'Having a Coke with You' and all this beautiful work, and about people who have written love letters, and found an apparatus of expression that's positive. It opened up the question of what it would mean to have a practice that remains wary of certain structures – that is still critical – but that can move beyond those structures to produce something that is... I don't know, mostly joy?

Q. THE WHITE REVIEW — Do you think that's how O'Hara wrote 'Having a Coke with You'?

A. CALLY SPOONER — Love letters are constructs: they are built, and engineered. Writing is engineering. I guess I'm learning the mechanics. It's a bit of an embarrassing process. I had this film on at the Stedelijk that took two years to make. It went through all these different phases, and loads of those phases I wish hadn't happened out loud, in public. Some of them I was proud of, some of them I wasn't, but I had to do them.

Q. THE WHITE REVIEW — Is working in public

like showing the mechanics of your love letters? How would you ideally have made the film?

A. CALLY SPOONER — Well I just am [working in public]. I couldn't have afforded to do it otherwise. The Stedelijk commissioned *AND YOU WERE WONDERFUL, ON STAGE* as a live piece for six women. It went to Performa and it grew to involve eighteen women, in a building that I moved an audience through. We did it five times. And then we did it at the Tate twice. By the second time at the Tate I felt that it didn't need to exist like this anymore. It was great that it happened, but it had turned into this really big show, and there was nothing more to learn. I then started to dismantle it, and think about how it could become something for camera. The film is the first and only take, unedited. It's a composite: each element had been rehearsed independently at different institutional shows, and made through different opportunities. It was all brought together at the Goodman studio in EMPAC, and the first time we brought every part together was the first take, and that's the film. So now I have a film, with all its fuck-ups and problems and mistakes. It's a choreography that happened just once and then disappeared, and it very nearly doesn't exist at all. It's fragile in that sense. That is really how I want to make work. The film still feels like it's living, I think.

Q. THE WHITE REVIEW — Does working in public change the end result? Would you have made a different film if it hadn't been through these iterations?

A. CALLY SPOONER — I don't know. I wish I felt as brave and powerful as Trisha Donnelly, who can negate everything for five years and say, 'It's still not ready.' I say 'yes' and then I use it to help me learn something that will help me do the thing I really want to do, like the film. That leaves a trail of things that I'm not so sure about, and it also means I work in public. I sometimes think that in an ideal world I would go quiet for two years and come back with something. But it's not true. The thing is, I love the film. I can only say that because there have been so many people working on it. I can't say that about a drawing I make on my own. I really love everyone who's in it, and I don't know whether they would all be in it if I hadn't made the film in the way I made it. It arrived in a certain way and that was the right way. I also think that I have always worked like that, even before my work involved a lot of hired people, a lot of performers, which is really expensive and mediated, and makes me less and less present, and more of an out-sourcer of sorts.

Q. THE WHITE REVIEW — Do you feel like a manager?

A. CALLY SPOONER — I feel like a manager and a carer, and a writer, a technocrat... I think if I were in another industry I would just be called a director, a film director. I don't like theatre. I kind of find theatre problematic, actually. I'm really into things happening at the very last possible moment, not something that's on tour, or is repeating itself. I'm not really interested in craftsmanship, in a star actor being able to 'channel the Dane' again. I'm interested in a group of people being really good at what they do, who have been learning something, coming together once and it never happening again. I find that really exciting.

Q. THE WHITE REVIEW — Because there is no good or bad night, no good or bad performance?

A. CALLY SPOONER — Exactly. It's about pro-duction. It landed where it landed. That's not to say it can't be critiqued, of course it can, but it can't be critiqued on the basis of in-dustrial design, or craftsmanship. I don't want to make theatre because I want to make something that's operating in the margins of last-minuteness, and is absolutely living. I'm much more into thinking about how to do something with people. It happens, and then we move on, because it's done. And then we disassemble.

Q. THE WHITE REVIEW — Why don't you usually film your live performances?

A. CALLY SPOONER — They're not choreo-graphed for a camera. They happen in the body of an audience, in the person next to you, in the acoustics of a space.

Q. THE WHITE REVIEW — And that audience is also part of the choreography? When you moved an audience through the Tate Britain for example, they weren't really separate from the hired performers.

A. CALLY SPOONER — It's a mulch of bod-ies. There is no stage. The choreography is language, it's writing, which organises the performing bodies and the viewing bodies in space.

Q. THE WHITE REVIEW — It's an atmosphere too. It's all happening in the air.

A. CALLY SPOONER — It's to do with rhythm, a rhythm that happens in space. Sometimes a piece of language needs to soar, or it needs to get impossible and then everyone disappears, and it's gone. Or it's empty, there's emptiness for a while, and then people throw voices across a building. This is all choreography, I think. That's why I consider them pieces of writing. I am a writer. That is the bottom line. I mean, I don't think I'm a very good writer, but it's the only thing I can be sure of. I un-derstand how to distribute language in a space.

And I can put on a live event. Beyond that I need to call someone.

At the Stedelijk I went with my sound engineer, Tom, to tune the space because I can't do it myself. I don't even know what he does but we have a conversation, he gets the idea of how the language needs to move in space. It's like he listens to the writing.

Q. THE WHITE REVIEW —— What about when you work with a dancer, for example – how important is it that they're professional?

A. CALLY SPOONER —— If there's a dancer that I'm working with I normally need them there to carry a particular register. In the Stedelijk film the dancers are producing this repetitious movement to a finale on a loop in their headsets. They're separate from everyone else. They produce this hypnotic image. I was thinking about them as a GIF almost, something that would keep your attention. I needed people to listen to the writing because the film has no centre or narrative. It was really important that the dancers were so good that you almost didn't notice them, and stayed locked into these rhythms and movements of the language rather than following a story. All the machinery and all the technical crew are visible in the film, and there isn't a hero or a plot – everyone and everything is a mechanic. You can hear me all the way through managing these mechanics. It's really important that they are professional because they just disappear – they are not an irksome tool. Likewise with the singers: it was necessary that it just *worked*. The voices end up becoming collapsed into one voice. That's why there are no male voices. They're all mezzos, so they gradually shift from difference to sameness.

Q. THE WHITE REVIEW —— The Vleeshal piece is quite different – the dynamic between dancers, but also because there is only movement, no language.

A. CALLY SPOONER —— It's a conceptual gesture, really – the 'work' in the work is a choreographic instruction. In that respect I think my work just got simpler, and my writing went somewhere else.

Q. THE WHITE REVIEW —— Do you want the writing to live somewhere else so you can figure out your relationship to these groups of people? Do you need to be straight up about being the administrator, rather than being everything – writer, manager, carer?

A. CALLY SPOONER —— I think so. My next project is making this company of sorts. I'm thinking about how it's possible to produce subjectivities in a group and in an audience, not just produce production. I don't actually know how to do that. I'm reading this book *HOW GOOGLE WORKS* [by Eric Schmidt and Jonathan Rosenberg] and it's like 'Have fun! Self-organise! Speak up! Be a team!' Saying, 'Everyone sends me emails saying how much they've loved working on my project' doesn't work any more, because it's exactly the same as being very happy to be a smart creative at Google. I want to spend a few years learning about management and directing so I don't go into another situation naively and accidentally reproduce the production space of *HOW GOOGLE WORKS* again. I'm looking at the mechanics and management that exist around industries and labour. Maybe that's my muse. Fuck, how depressing. I'd rather have a better muse than the misery of immaterial labour.

Q. THE WHITE REVIEW —— Like a really attractive human.

A. CALLY SPOONER —— That's why I cried.

Q. THE WHITE REVIEW — Of course you did! Your muse is oppressive by nature!

A. CALLY SPOONER — So now I'm thinking about how I can restructure my writing so I can be more present in it.

Q. THE WHITE REVIEW — As in, your voice?

A. CALLY SPOONER — Yes, my voice. I never really have anything to say. I never really know what to say. I don't have a message. I'm more like Hannah Arendt than William Burroughs. I'm sitting at my desk, reading. I'm not traversing around with some heroin. I love writing, but I mean, I hate it. I'm terrible at it. It's horrible, isn't it? But I love to hear writing read out loud. And I love it when it gets put into other people's bodies and it finds this... life. I think it's life-affirming. It's better that it happens than it doesn't.

When I was working on *And You Were Wonderful, On Stage*, I wrote the script for a show at Camberwell Space and then that was it, I was in professional mode. I was auditioning people, then I was going to all these places, and I didn't write anything for eighteen months. Invitations came to do shows, and I don't have a whole lot of ideas. I don't want a whole lot of ideas.

Q. THE WHITE REVIEW — You mean you don't have a list of ideas, of shows you want to do?

A. CALLY SPOONER — Not at all! I have books that I'm reading and things that I've watched and people I've met and instincts about something I hear on the radio, or how I want something to feel. I'll be obsessed with a sound I've heard in a Gregory Whitehead radio play: how did he do that? I have these things floating around but I don't have 'ideas'. That's a problem when you get invited to do shows: you have to come up with an 'idea'. *And You Were Wonderful, On Stage* protected me

in that sense, because every time I was invited to do a show I would make a prop or a piece of choreography, but it meant I was in production for a really long time. Now I'm trying to find a way of delivering works that I'm proud of, a space that's more intimate. I've started drawing, and I've been making these paperweights... [Opens a box that's been sitting on the desk] It's my ear! I've been making these big stacks of my writing held down by these paperweights in the shape of my ear.

Q. THE WHITE REVIEW — I can't see a disembodied ear without the mouse attached.

A. CALLY SPOONER — You can grow anything! It's kind of depressing. The ear is this super important tool when being a manager and being managed. It is also this really intimate, erotic space. For the show in Texas I had stacks of paper – the start of a novel. There was just a drawing and these stacks of writing held down by these ears. I was really happy with that. I felt really present in it. It's really simple and it would have been nothing without the writing.

Q. THE WHITE REVIEW — Everything was in the service of the writing?

A. CALLY SPOONER — Exactly. I'm scared about the New Museum because it's this big show in New York, but I want to keep it very very simple. I need to make sure that I can find a space to write alongside the work itself. I think I've found it actually: I'm in the catalogue, I wrote there. I'm very happy there. I just need to find the performers now. I don't know why but the right people always come along, so maybe I should just shut up and let it happen.

ALICE HATTRICK, FEBRUARY 2016

PONY: FIVE TABLEAUX

BY

SOPHIE SEITA

‹NOW SEND A MESSAGE TO THE OBJECT›

‹MYTH›

the periphery only seems closer
it's a trick
they're watching
to count steps

stars and mermaids praise and sing their chariot fevers
until the last plonk
it's a great song
carolled by a pony

i shall build my pony a bed in a shoebox
garner it gold–purple, maybe orange
the pony probably wants booze and sperm but i shall not let it

there is no world after objects. or so they say
they who are in this world, luxuriate in memories, penetrate surfaces
like they were milk skin which is common
as a form of denaturation, when you apply external stress
to a living cell it causes death. and so it does

men are talking. i do not need to give numbers
only reflected rendering

looking into her hand mirror my pony is female and pretty

＊

Pony is a universe of captivated life
its being held unmoved in petrified activity steals outside our borders of time

aesthetic littleness is a mantelpiece a stunned materiality
a private entrancement on a wide meadow with a sustained star
the lower business of the vision of the allegory
of the stilled vision timed stillness is also social and gigantic

giants are grotesque. as souvenirs they pertain.
always bashful or timorous Pony is mini in their control of resources and pleasure

*

i call Pony, the real patrol, which doesn't exist, which undoes itself,
that is only one of Pony's acknowledgements, we could call them rejoinders

where's Pony in the great american novel?

jody never waited for the triangle to get him out of bed after the coming of the red pony

Pony did not talk with the ears, what a stupid idea

and he felt the pony's legs and tested the heat of the flanks. he put his cheek against
the pony's gray muzzle and then he rolled up the eyelids to look at the eyeballs and
he lifted the lips to see the gums, and he put his fingers inside the ears

this is called fiction

<SONG>

you will have a song, Pony, a little song a little air a little ditty sweet weather as a
wager, you will have a song, Pony, gleam gleam chip tin and ting maybe clink
and clank, uiii, a little life not at all new to you says who, say hi to the patrimony
which is a good padre almost holy, this is how it is

i call Pony I tell her:
        you can make actions that seem difficult more immediate by placing an
        'i wish' before them

the example is every boy is riding a pony
which children understand to mean always
in the domain of quantification

quantifiers are spreading   naturally
no one questioned the boys
the presupposed set of individuals

sometimes we say each man is carrying a box
sometimes all men are watching
        the stars

hey, says Pony, compare: this coherence is totally fabricated
the stargazer who slumbered dogmatically is with us still, now inveigh
against the deep, the fumbling creatures are *held*,
these are just acts of imagination with respect to the pony

<DIALOGUE>

i: hello.
Pony: hello.

i: let's do that again.
Pony: ok.

i: hello.
Pony: hello.

Pony: different?
i: maybe.

i: i've forgotten the instructions.
Pony: that's sad.
i: it's not real.
Pony: ah.

it's an easy gesture, i use it often and expertly
i have no such options with the pony

*

action choices:

avoid the truth
avoid delicate matters
avoid being tracked down

instead chew up and spit it out
then carry out an important mission

a pony is queen of delicate matters
and says, i shall not cut through the fog love the world be suitable

and the pony leaves to examine its folly, to excite someone,
to go where no man has gone before,

it induces, it listens, it rattles up some shit,
can't have it both ways,

     Pony, liberating the oppressed, jumps at chances, picks out the jewels
in its crown, for it wears a crown, having killed the queen and stolen her
ornaments. jewels in hands, or rather hooves, the pony leaps, and
disperses the riches, puts the world in order, sings charitable progress,
this is no exaggeration

Pony is victorious. the pony has no record of losing

    *

how does the object fulfil your wishes?
how does it serve you?

one way to acknowledge servitude would be to say:
there is a charm bracelet wandering over your body

pony has no cutie marks
her brand is unprofitable

a way to test your character is to put it in a situation away from the text
and into contexts which have to do with money. let's see

pony is not a character, not an alias, but a quintessence, an iridescence
conferred.

in this metaphor one is using the pony discreetly
is the transition the moment of fragment of translation

this is not a story about a pony

*

the pony tries to understand the glitter, the plastic, and the purple lock
not being human what it means to count words to know numbers to read relations
speak truthfully and in an ethical stance

divisions and quotations, sideways exceptions and more words,
words are endless it is tiresome, sigh

the pony is perfect because it is not proper
of its kind in size and kind, it is not-yet, not-quite right

*she was a regular pony and I put a flamey, hearty symbol on her and called her
Burning Love.*

the conditions of our pact were unclear
let's hold our arms still, the pony says. this is how things'll get better
juggle, don't worry (a borrowed tranquility)
pony has wings, it is capable of flight, it can sustain it,
it has power through a wink

the pony confessed to me and it wasn't nice
i didn't know what i was getting into

there was no warning, no education
it was pure ideology. excuse the vocabulary
i mean it was shiny hair and big eyes and pinkishness and delightful smiles
pinkish-yellow glow it is the stardust snap and crackle perhaps moondust?
which is glitter which is beauty

    all ponies are girls

<HYPOTHESIS I>

living pictures animate
actors mimic tables
i mean tableaux

the collector examines, sounds out these bodies, frozen, cracked sometimes
in tiny movements that disturb the order of representation
to illuminate some mysteries, to puncture secrets

the collector evacuates and absorbs mysteries in hypotheses
through imagined stolen paintings
nesting their complaints, their history

some say the pony is the most judicious of creatures
some call it a hold-up artist, an outlaw, a chiseller,
i see no contradiction in this

<HYPOTHESIS 2>

thieves held up the stolen painting. it glimmered in the light
they supported it with one hand while balancing on the beam
someone watched them

what's holding that mirror?

chiselling away at the most statuesque of its likeness
the pony was still, it was held still, it did not move,
its posture resembled that of a woman

rolling rocks up mountains, walking steps in small scale
but held unmoved
how statuesque they say

the stolen one held the belief embodied the belief
in the graceful the shapely the tall

a statue is never little

and so they mumble stupidly as is expected:

*never yet did my eye light upon a creature more matchless in its proportions, more
statuesque.*

we could call this pony's table talk
we all know that animals perform heroic deeds
and ponies are divinatory, they warn of danger

*

searching for notorious reception
through an ill-fated exhibition they educate inside the fragment
the diegesis, the centre of gravity richly and preciously grouped together
they droop the poses

P

when the album was completed around and showed the statues in all their
faces in public crowded into a dark room, curtains closed, they had another
table, and it was time to start again après. après coup. when the disc had
completed a lap and looks showed the statues in all their faces in public
occasions crowded into the shady scopes, the curtain was closing

so the table is an allegory of the future as if i had to tell you

a more precisely located moment like
the irreparable gesture
the action suspended, put in 'pose'
would be more probable and
points towards a convergence–a clandestine ceremony–
a ceremonial puzzle
a fragmentary window

indecipherable in the absence of seriality
the critically missing link is the indefinable object

in covert medieval fraternities, the orders of knights
are cognitive aberrations implicit in the knowable and articulate
a crazy hypothesis
in such exquisitely formalised poise

it is a pleasure to find that, although many nude pictures are realised, there is not a
suspicion of indelicacy

sometimes a poem accompanies the scene
sometimes a wooden frame steers peripherally

if the pedigree is thus sometimes accomplished with regret, it cylinders also in
    ecstasy
this word is not too much. i fancy Pony is 'happy'.
sit venia verbo
the remark is sacred and heavy to bear

again:
when sometimes something crucial misses in the series how do we read it
conjecture is the tool of the damned
it's ceremony that makes up textbook circular curves

    the simulation of held life

*

here i present you the pose plastique, the pregnant moment
the costumed table
just some colloquial phrase

living as fish in a vivarium, nouns in a linguistic study
to think of a third agency in this relationship
is an example contemplating circumstance

imagine for a moment a party
endlessly stylish, initially optimistic
silence broken by delighted guess–games
innocent amusements for the young
then intense physical control

according to contemporary sources
you apprehend the ideal when
silent and immobile in imitation

are the stars, as stars

they observe

sometimes they are dreamers, i.e. they are given the utopic scale

we have the fresh graces we are elected to demonstrate
eager to replicate the fashions and follies
enough to warrant criticism,

P

the birth of society brings
spaciousness and order so lovingly shrill
fabulously dull, or hung, which is the trap
too too fully in another, mostly into, ah, yes,
so funky and savvy
they form choruses, in feline opulence—
adjectives are myth

*

let's return succinctly to the pony

what can be a variable, a location in memory, also an instance of class
this is by way of summary so we speak the same language

is pony an object
is pictured
is stolen
is hidden from sight

thought is directed towards it
what are its attributes its capacity for beginning
perhaps it is already written and copied and described
but a system integrates patterns at creation time
a fixed state of transactions via the operator who knows and does too much
whose sole purpose is restriction

an object that contains other objects

clues, noting a cover-up, on the side of the reference 'in here',
is the need of the mind in the construction of importance
conspiracy is the signal. throw a gap by simply opening. and wear it
allegedly
allegedly
allegedly
withdrawn and unreadable by chance

the formation of a hypothesis is senseless
conveys the banality with a touch of mystery and excitement
subtraction tests are bad
as the addition of absence

tableaux are data subjected to measurements, begging isolation of an object

at first wretched and reckonable but truly splendid and unknown
in a single inheritance
a world assumption
in a lisp

DON'T CALL 'EM BUSTS, THEY'RE TORSOS PEOPLE

BY

AMY BESSONE

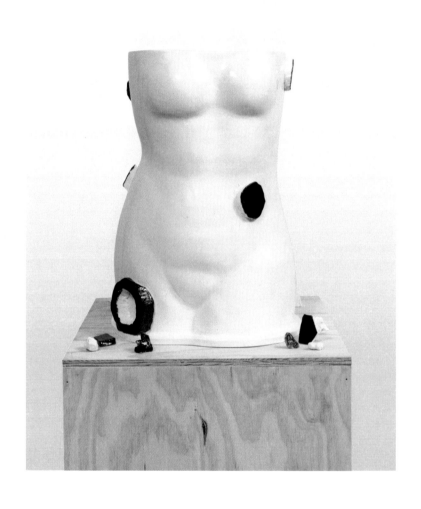

FLYING TO THE INTERIOR

BY

MARTIN MACINNES

1.

Amateur ornithological associations tagged carrion birds as a way of tracking feed–
ing and mating behaviours. In the project's ten–year span several spikes were noted
– short periods when unusually high numbers of birds congregated in the same
area. Many of these events were found to correlate with the timings of unexplained
disappearances of light aircraft.

2.

Balloonists prepared cross–Pacific journeys, documenting every step of the process
online until the official launch date. A period of silence followed lasting between two
and three months, after which it was announced that the flight had not yet begun.
Adjustments were made to the original reports, explaining the delays to the expedition
launch. In the drafts of the documentary record discrepancies emerged relating to the
number of people believed to be taking part in the ascent – first six, then three, then
finally one. The record continued to be revised over the next several years as further,
more ambitious expeditions with new balloonists were planned and then deleted.
Each time, in the run–up to the scheduled launch date, all reports confidently stated
that the balloon would now ascend. Numerous blog posts were posted along with
media interviews, photographic journals and short films explaining the technical
operation of the flight. Doctors and dieticians described what would happen to the
body at each respective height, how it would be replenished and stabilised against the
changing pressure and temperature of the atmosphere. Marine geographers explained
in detail the nature of the water crossed and experts in rainforest ecology described
the life present in the canopy terrain of South America and Asia which comprised the
planned launch and landing sites. As each new launch date approached the problems
affecting previously scheduled balloon flights, forcing multiple postponements, were
laid out in some detail, and hired actors read confidently from scripts prepared by
technical staff stating clearly why now, finally – this time – the balloon could be
airborne, the crossing would be made.

3.

Rumours were spread on in–house message boards by coders in Guyana and
encrypted into economic predictions by financiers in Brasilia relating to the practice
of 'urban marches'. Administrative workers in middle age walked alone out of the
office at midday, carrying only basic supplies – sandwiches, pasta, sliced fruit, 0.5 litre
bottles of water, suit jackets. They were to walk as far as was possible into the interior
of the country, avoiding all use of public transport and organised accommodation and
eschewing any human communication. Men and women known as exiles modelled
their journeys on sixth–century monks drifting thousands of miles on rafts directed

by ephemeral voices, whale-song, and atmospheric pressures, possibly discovering archipelagoes and whole continents hundreds of years before government missions did. They drank river water and ate fruit, insects, and bird nests, walking further into forest and marshland. Sedentary colleagues alluded to their journeys in impenetrable legalese and in long financial reports that would never be read. Large sums of company money were invested betting on which individual would achieve the greatest distance, and who would be the first to make it out the other side, past the interior, rather than ultimately retracing outward steps on the long homeward journey. In-house, these extended leave periods were referred to as performance improvement sabbaticals or stress-related time away. Returning exiles quickly ascended to senior corporate positions and generally established a family including a stay-at-home wife and at least one mistress.

4.

Over six days and 1,500 square miles of rainforest forty-six reports were made to emergency services, local media outlets and churches regarding visitations of saints and angels in trees. The epicentre was established as an agrarian commune – a quarantine was put up. The previous day all associated livestock had died having shown no prior signs of disease. The surrounding flora began to dry, degrade, fold and collapse; epidemiology experts discovered that all insect life in the commune had disappeared, the vegetation dying as a direct result.

All twenty-three members of the commune were imprisoned and interrogated, suspected of collusion in a pre-terrorist plot. The site was meticulously searched for evidence of the toxins responsible. The commune members maintained innocence until their respective pain thresholds were met, at which point they invented what they hoped would be a sufficient story. The stories were mutually incompatible, bearing no coherent thread. Flashes of white light were reported near the upper canopy around the time the livestock died. Noting the absence of birdlife from the area government advisors re-routed the flight paths of all aircraft due to fly within a 500-mile radius. In a 400-page report, subsequent to a spontaneous wildfire destroying the entirety of the commune, administrators avoided using the words 'non-terrestrial pathogens' and 'site of awe'.

5.

NASA-sourced heat-imaging technology floating on balloons over the forest revealed inexplicable concentrations of unknown mammalian forms. Given the nature of the recording equipment it was impossible to identify the beginning and ending of bodies, and so the warm life-cloud, moving in an approximately unitary manner, could not be identified by species. It was estimated that if the bodies were human then the number was 200. Tracking body heat, the movement was seen to be regularly slow with infrequent bouts of extreme speed. No communities were recognised as existing in the area. Government sponsored 'tribal reconciliation' missions had previously charted the adjacent land to significant distances in every direction. Trusted cartel representatives assured ministers of their ignorance – products were harvested and hostages maintained in clearly defined and officially sanctioned areas. Such was the density of the canopy, satellite- and drone-supplied images were rendered redundant; nevertheless all footage was exhaustively examined.

Tracking all records of activity in the area a technician noted a missile launch centre abandoned 200km north-east of the heat cloud's present location. The site had trialled experimental, non-petroleum fuel sources and innovative propulsion technology, but the results were insignificant and any equipment worth less than the cost of extraction was left to melt into the roots, vines and animals of the forest floor.

In the sole survey of the site biologists had noted moderately unusual rates of floral growth as well as several newly discovered and endemic symbiotic relationships. The identity of the mammalian forms was never established.

6.

Automated checks on flights missing, believed crashed, over the forest in the past two decades brought up statistically unlikely repetitions. Of the nineteen flights still unaccounted for, sixteen carried men and women flying on return tickets that chronologically contradicted their journey. The return journey, in the case of one person on each of these flights, was scheduled to take place while the outward flight remained in progress. The age of these passengers ranged from 27 to 42, origin was local and ethnicity caucasian, and the stated purpose of travel, every time, was 'business'. They all worked for a series of small corporations linked to a larger umbrella unit whose remit remained unknown. It was proved, in thirteen of the sixteen cases, that the passenger in question had at least some experience piloting small aircraft.

Independent enthusiasts investigated these figures and the circumstances of each missing flight. Rumours spread and people became suspicious of briefcases carried on small planes scheduled to fly over the interior. It was advised to dress in informal clothes. Increasingly elaborate and outrageous rumours circulated. Online forums proliferated; for each one pulled down another three sprang up. It was claimed a mechanised belt, 11 miles long, was built into the forest and covered in inauthentic, permanently preserved flora. When activated, the belt moved backwards, revealing a long strip of runway. The figure – the affiliated employee – on each flight allegedly forced command of the aircraft and landed on the artificial strip. Possible reasons for bringing the flights in were various, and disputed: it was the material contained in the suitcase; it was the identity, rather, of another of the passengers, who worked as a foreign operative and possessed valuable information relating to a new technology, which would itself then be built in the forest, using the materials of the dismantled aircraft, under the supervision of the interrogated and re-educated foreign operative; it was the aircraft itself, kept hidden under the forest belt, used to spray experimental poisons over small and unsuspecting indigenous communities; it was the passenger cargo, freely incarcerated deep in the vast forest, monitored remotely as they attempted to come to terms with their situation, remaining sedentary or planning a long escape, isolating themselves or forging alliances, making peace with the strangely impassive captors or waging futile war – they were placed, members of the passenger cargo, into artificial situations, put into uncomfortable domestic and dramatic arrangements, offered rewards or punishment according to how naturally they played along. The more aircrafts that were taken, and the greater the number of conditioned passenger cargo, the quicker the newly landed adapted to forest life.

Some of the first to be captured, who had reacted violently and rebelled for years, became among the most valuable of those present at the base, playing a key role in convincing the newcomers how fortunate they were to be there, how exciting the project was. Generations of people were born in the sprawling campsite, raised with only specific planted knowledge about the 'outside world'. Many situations were run, in the camp buildings, constructed from flat-pack materials contained in the suitcases and from everything that had previously composed the aircraft, from the wings to the head-rests, the toilet-seats to the trays the re-heated food had been presented on. The idea was that the camp would in time run organically, autonomously, as the younger generations, those who had been born in the environment, grew to maturation and learned to command. New arrivals came periodically – the rolling out of the 11-mile belt and the landing of the unfamiliar object were built into the community's mythology. The reality behind the situation – that this was an artificially constructed community illegally planted in the forest, that none of them belonged there and that the scenes of their lives were scripted simulations – became only one among many of the fantasies popular with the younger and idler camp members. Other fantasies entertained included that each member of the camp had come there via water, swimming a period of approximately 4.58 billion years, this being only the second leg of an even longer journey largely involving darkness, sudden rapid and inexplicable inflations and the serial arrival of massive, spinning light bodies. They were very tired after that journey but at the same time exhilarated, both jaded and anxious to begin, and in the tension between these states they lived approximately sixty-seven years each.

New languages were developed, old ones filtered out, and on each new landing the incomers, when they opened their mouths, were treated with righteous, furious disgust: their words were a disease and their mouths would be broken and re-set.

F

Speculations over the ultimate purpose behind everything – the corporate involvement from the very beginning the bringing down of the aircrafts the willingness of sixteen men and women at least to overhaul their lives, leaving families and friends behind, and taking over 1,000 individuals forcibly captive in the forest, the huge expenditure involved in the operation, the meticulous planning and the enormous energy invested from the start – were similarly various. Many of the theories centred on the commercial advantages likely gained by the company ultimately responsible, the usefulness of the vast amounts of anthropological data gathered in watching how these people lived, day in and day out, in situations that were prompted and invented by those ultimately in control. The commercial benefit of insights gained was considered incalculable – in research and development, in marketing strategy, in product design – and in one sense this may have been deemed enough for establishing the simulated society with all that it entailed.

A closely related group of theories claimed a religio–corporate remit for the establishing of the artificial world, the compound being prepared as a new beginning ready to step in after the inevitable implosion of larger, linked urban areas. After running for 1,000 years, having utilised materials collected from increasingly sophisticated aircraft, and after a sufficient period of silence, the corporate compound would move outwards to the coast, build satellite communities, cross water, establish an increased rate of reproduction and ultimately colonise the world.

Those in positions of authority dictated domestic arrangements, work routines, and available leisure activities. Apparently indiscriminately, people were removed from their everyday lives and transplanted into another building where they lived with a new family, worked a different job, and were called by an alternative name. Children were raised according to alternating philosophies, a first–born being told that they were a frail organism decaying at an increasing rate and a second believing that experience, folded into memory, is endless. People tried to escape in new ways. Smoke balloons, their fabric stitched from tens of thousands of small patches torn from clothing, lifted children no more than 17 miles from camp, at which point they returned for food. Several generations of a single family, some of whom had never met, worked together on a narrow tunnel leading west from beneath the front room in their home building. In order to reach a significant distance a single individual was required to live underground, tunnelling, for extended periods, which involved considerable practical difficulties. To provide food and drink one male and one female white mouse were tethered together on the end of a 2–foot stick – the tunneller utilised their high reproductive yield as a source of milk and meat, consuming many generations of a direct familial line. The generations became increasingly tame and docile, living with limited freedom and in the dark, subsisting on black beetles and ants. In eleven generations the rope used to tether the mice became redundant, as they were now

programmed to move in line with the human tunneller and to provide them with
the necessary meat and milk. Their brains reduced in size accordingly, unnecessary
energy expended on maintaining obsolete functions deemed too costly. Relatives of
the tunneller currently chosen would take turns, on the surface, impersonating the
missing, so that the extended period of absence would not be noted. Each tunneller
would typically spend one year digging east before crawling backwards through
blood, faeces, urine and expired mice, and exchanging places. After forty years'
tunnelling, when it was finally decided to dig upwards and emerge, the 29-year-
old man currently occupying the role looked around him in some surprise. He was
confident, as he rose, that they had built a path so far from home captivity that he had
reached some kind of edge – perhaps the ocean. In the tunnel aural hallucination was
common but he was certain the concussion heard above was really waves. He would
fell a tree, use vines as twine and sail to a port to contact the world, the real world, the
bigger world, and the whole artificial construct that he and his family and everybody
he had known were brought up in would collapse.

As he broke the surface his vision fizzed. The light slowly drifted back into sense,
form and specificity and he saw his family sitting together at the table and apparently
enjoying a meal. They looked at him in some confusion. He was struck by the details
of the objects in the room. Plastic white cutlery separated neatly into Tupperware
containers. Foam-backed seats set directly onto the earthen floor. A table made from
differently coloured fabric stitched together, supporting his family's heads and elbows.
He had seen every one of these objects uncountable times before, but as they had been
the last things he expected to see, hundreds if not thousands of miles from home, they
were amazing. Somehow all of this – the family scene – had been extracted, lifted
and transported to the land-edge. They were there to meet him as he emerged, and
it was the last thing he expected. There was a knock on the door, and a community
leader entered. She explained that the family, over three generations, had charted a
significant area of forest, but that rather than leading due east as they had intended,
and as they had started out and believed they continued, they had actually traced what
had become a perfect circle, unconsciously following the apparent direction of the
sun and returning inevitably home. What is more, the community leader informed
them, there is no reason for you to do this underground, you are more than welcome
to attempt such an escape on the surface, it will be safer that way. None of us will stop
you. Rest assured, you will not be watched or hunted. Nevertheless we are confident
that you will ultimately choose to return here, the place you belong.

❡ Another explanation for what happened to the missing aircraft was that the corporate
identities taking hold of the controls deliberately crash-landed over particularly dense
coverage. The cruising speed, altitude and fuel levels were calculated to optimally

facilitate a 'soft crash' – a particular form of mechanical free-falling in which the aircraft and its cargo are not immolated or otherwise entirely obliterated on contact with the ground.

Typically less than a third of the cargo survive, and the injuries are substantial. For months individuals may subsist high in the trees on leaves, insect larvae and rainwater. Others suffer multiple fractures and amputations on impact with the ground. Significant trauma-induced amnesia combined with dramatic physical injuries, at times recasting the whole anatomy of the living human, puts the identity in a state supremely suggestible to environmental and imaginative cues – anatomical displacements enabling increased flexibility, lesions on the brain causing curiously adaptive psychological disturbances. Ex-academy anthropologists were quoted stating heterodox opinions on the viability, under such extreme conditions, of a 'reversion' to pre-linguistic modes of living: shifts in diurnal settings leading to the development of nocturnal hunting behaviour; landing impacts on hip and spinal areas forcing quadruped locomotion, arboreal sleeping, and increased communion with animals; loss of medium- and long-term memory causing disintegration of selfhood and abandonment of narrative and time. Pictures were drawn of survivor communities existing in a state of flux, pre-cultural, rapacious, successful. There were stories of these people, formidable hunters, working less and less in tandem with each other, favouring a voiceless, pre-cooperative method of society, meeting only periodically, seasonally, to copulate in mass events. Men began experimenting with other organisms. Some emerged as 'guest' members of smaller primate troops, accommodated for the advantages of their unusual dexterity, but ejected, usually killed and eaten, because of the severe war-like and proprietary elements structured deep within their behaviour. The ex-humans also, occasionally, activated the larynx and diaphragm and made strange, loud, prolonged nasal expressions which frightened the other animals and disrupted their hunts, these episodes occurring exclusively in the night, when they were forced down and the salted emissions were licked from their faces.

SCROLL, SKIM, STARE

BY

ORIT GAT

I.

This is an essay about contemporary art that includes no examples. It includes no examples because its subject – artists' websites, their form and function, and the possibilities they hold – is prone to constant change. This text is an attempt to document a thing always fleeting – the aesthetics of the web – without fixing it, since it begins with a concern about growing uniformity and ends with a call for change.

The web has redefined research in the visual arts: sifting through images online. The proliferation of images on the internet has changed the way we look at art because we are exposed to an unprecedented deluge of images online. The visual literacy developed as a result informs both the making and viewing of art, but it has not chipped away at the primacy of the gallery or museum as the site for encountering it. The physical experience of viewing art is, nonetheless, different as a result of the way we use the internet: the body in the gallery space engages with the work by way of selfies, by way of directing a camera. The result, however, is the further addition of images to an internet already full to the brim.

To paraphrase Croatian artist Mladen Stilinović's 1994 banner embroidered with the claim that 'an artist who cannot speak English is no artist', today one could say that a young artist who doesn't have a website is no artist. Stilinović comes to mind because his maxim is a statement about access and the prerequisites for participation in the art industry. English still dominates, but today there's also the stipulation to participate in the image culture online. For an artist to have a website is almost a generational marker: many artists who came to prominence in the 1980s and 1990s settle for a Wikipedia entry or a page on their gallery's website. It's not that they have no stake in how their work is presented online, simply that since they rose to prominence before having a website was the norm (not to say requirement), they never caught up. Though the state and place of art on the internet is a matter of concern for all artists, critics, curators, dealers, and viewers, direct engagement via personal websites is at the moment undertaken by younger or emerging artists who are more likely to contribute to – and control – the presentation of their works online. These artists can change the way we look at art online.

Could artists' websites disrupt or shape the contemporary image economy, the current state of visual culture on the internet which is defined by hypercirculation, overexposure and low attention spans? Right now, the conformity of artists' websites is surprising considering the variety of artistic approaches, mediums, and styles in contemporary art. This is not reflected in artists' websites: a small number of platforms such as Indexhibit and Cargo Collective are used by a large majority of artists when building their sites, responding to a checklist of unchanging components (CV, contact information, images). The consequence is that artists' websites rarely do justice to their work.

This essay is not a call to artists to hire designers who will build them custom-made sites (though that kind of collaboration could be fruitful for both). Instead, it looks at the artist's website as what it could be: an online exhibition platform. This would provide an alternative to the static presentations of installation shots from conventional galleries that are, unaccountably, the dominant mode of presenting contemporary art on the web. We are living through the peak moment of social media, and the construction of one's image online is a chewed-up topic, but the artist's website could be different – it could offer a new way of participating in visual culture online, it could delineate a new form. The issue at stake in this essay is not only how artists can show their work, but also how these displays reflect the way we see art today and the current state of visual research.

2.

On 16 September 2014, Sir Tim Berners-Lee – the computer scientist credited with the invention of the World Wide Web at CERN, the European Organisation for Nuclear Research in Geneva, in 1989 – tweeted a link to internet Live Stats, a live counter created by a group of developers, researchers and analysts who collect and present live data about use of the web. The tweet celebrated a milestone: one billion websites. Internet Live Stats is almost hypnotic: it's a list of categories organised by day or by second. The site counts how many internet users there are (a guesstimate: around the time this text will be printed it will be about 3.5 billion); how many emails were sent on the day you looked at the site; how many Google searches were made; blog posts written; emails sent; tweets published; videos viewed on YouTube and so on. It would be futile to quote any number from the site because, as I write this, I can see numbers changing. But here's one: as of February 2016, 486 Instagram photos are uploaded every second. That's over 40 million images a day. And that's just Instagram, just one source of images uploaded to the internet. Every two minutes, people upload more photographs to the internet than existed in total just 150 years ago (and this information is correct as of 2014). This proliferation has changed the condition of viewing images today in a way as monumental as the advent of photography or the introduction of illustrated newspapers in the mid-nineteenth century.

Contemporary art is all over the internet. It is found on Google Images; it's featured on sites meant to sell work, like the online marketplace Artsy and the online auction house Paddle8; it is disseminated via numerous 'one image a day' sites, curated by artists or viewers; video art is streamed on different platforms, some legal, some not; art is featured on Instagram, Twitter, Facebook; it's in the online newspaper and magazine. In all of these different spaces, the artworks travel accompanied by different levels of context. On social media they are framed by publics, both the people who originally posted them (either in an art space or by reposting an image found elsewhere online) and their followers. In different discursive programmes like online magazines or newspapers' websites they often join reportage. On the marketplace websites they are accompanied by information concerning specific pieces' provenance, sale histories, and price. These artworks are often tagged and categorised by medium, and are rarely unique images, but rather, copies of copies of existing JPEGs whose origins are often hard to pinpoint.

This means that contemporary art is inseparable from the current image economy in a variety of ways, first and foremost the fact that art now circulates as JPEGs – that the media of documentation has become the thing itself. This is perfectly exemplified in one popular website, Contemporary Art Daily. Its white background and unvaryingly sized images have become an accepted way of looking at and circulating art online. At least once a day, the site features a series of installation shots from gallery exhibitions around the world, accompanied by the press release. The selection of shows gravitates towards a certain generation of young galleries in Europe and the United States, and the images conform to a particular aesthetic: art on Contemporary Art Daily is always shown within the same familiar environment, including white walls, cement floors, overhead lights. Its mission statement reads, 'Contemporary Art Group advances important art and improves the public's access to it through curated programming and the development of archives.' The organisation is a not-for-profit meant to promote access to and visibility of art, but its straight-up translation of the white cube format into the online presentation of art means the art Contemporary Art Daily promotes adheres to value structures built in brick-and-mortar galleries, and is passed around as such. Rather than images of the work, we get images of the work in a building; rather than an expansion of the ways art circulates online, it is an expansion of the tried-and-tested commercial model.

Art – like all cultural production – has a complicated status online. It becomes 'content', that catchall phrase for the stuff that advertising is sold around. And that is also the condition in which art is viewed: as part of a mass. An emblematic example of the accumulation of imagery on the web is 4chan. Started by Christopher Poole in 2003 and still going strong, 4chan is an online community revolving around imageboards, digital spaces where people communicate by sharing images. 4chan's members are in charge of too many memes that have gone viral for anyone to count, and at some point hacked the *TIME* magazine Person of the Year 'people's choice' award, giving it to Poole. Theirs is an internet of jokes, visual cues, repetition, and hyper circulation. The infamy of 4chan is the result of its virality, but also of its pace, which, with dozens of images posted by the minute, is emblematic of the way we think of image economies on the internet.

At the moment, few online outlets challenge this primacy of the image. Quite the opposite: the design of web-based magazines and other sites typically privileges images and video over text. This tendency responds to attention economies online – viewers scroll, skim, allow video autoplay. One of the few origins of the dominance of text in the early internet – search engine optimisation – is losing traction with the development of image-recognition software. The result is an ecology of soundbites, of the quick-to-consume, a publishing environment that seems so inherent to the internet it is rarely challenged.

3.
Indexhibit is a web app content management system (CMS) created by artist Daniel Eatock and graphic designer Jeffery Vaska in 2006, designed to allow artists to set up their own websites. It was free until 2012 and is currently offered at the modest one-time cost of €25 (and €75 for a company). The do-it-yourself ethos of Indexhibit is evident on its homepage, where it reads 'Created by Daniel Eatock, Jeffery Vaska, and you'. The platform is simple and easy to use, so much so that at some point in the early 2010s it seemed ubiquitous among artists. As a result, artists' websites came to look the same: a list of links on the left (the typeface is usually blue), which expand on the main area to the right. This structure is what Indexhibit draws its name from: index+exhibit. From its About page: 'The Indexhibit format has become archetypal for the creative community, combining good functionality and usability for the website maker and visitors.'

Though 10 years old, Indexhibit is still prominent among artists looking to build websites, even as other modules have gained popularity at the expense of the index format. Typical are the grid of thumbnail images (a popular template on another favoured platform, Cargo) and the blogroll – the scroll-down through posts, reverse-chronology design often built using established publishing platforms like Wordpress and Tumblr. This might read like a list of service providers, but it shouldn't: these are the structures through which contemporary art is viewed today.

The design of an artist's website contextualises production. Just as the white cube (optional: polished concrete floors, skylights) is a recognisable, sanctioned structure for viewing contemporary art, so the list of links on the left or the grid of thumbnail images have come to define the artist's website. In both cases, the visitor discerns that this is a space for contemporary art; in both, the architecture defines the viewing experience. Just as paintings look great against white walls with overhead lights, so a series of thumbnails communicates a certain brand of visual art, which is object-oriented and emphasises cohesion, since viewing the grid of thumbnail images or cropped details delivers consistency of vision.

The index+exhibit format also encourages artists to taxonomise their work by project: since the links on the left stand in for a collection of texts and images that will unfold to the right of the index, it lends itself better to combining series of works or

E

different aspects of a project under one link. The blogroll, often presented in reverse-chronological order, encourages an additive presentation reliant on constant updating and thus more dependent on tags to create connections between newer posts and the older ones that may disappear down the site.

These three dominant designs are different approaches to information architecture. None of these are groundbreaking or revolutionary but they define the way viewers experience art. They mirror contemporary production, especially in the case of Indexhibit, which reflects the fact that an increasing number of artists are working on a project–by–project basis, whether because they are working other jobs, or because their work requires travel or expensive materials, or because they rely on residencies to find time to produce.

The above taxonomies were not imposed on art by lazy design, but these formats give them the monotony of grocery lists: CV, contact information, news, images. The sites channel an outmoded form: the portfolio, those black folders compiling prints or works on paper encased in nylon, surrounded by title pages and sometimes a single-paragraph explanation of each work. A website enables the creation of portfolios much more attuned to the varied forms and practices of contemporary art, whether embedded video, multiple installation shots for three–dimensional works, audio for sound pieces, download STL files for limitless editions of 3D–printed work, video tours of exhibitions, archival matter, research materials and other process–oriented examples, or simply high–resolution, zoomable details for paintings.

But an artist's website could be more than this, even. Aside from those working directly on digital culture – creating websites, apps, and videos meant to be experienced on a computer or mobile device – few artists today think about their websites as exhibition platforms, when in fact an artist's website allows for an inordinate amount of freedom and experimentation to present that work to its best advantage to a wide audience. It is also a rare space in which artists can control the way their work is presented. Unlike the series of thumbnails that is Google Images or a museum or gallery's website, which foreground the way the work looked when it was exhibited in the physical exhibition space, on a personal site any artist can choose to present their work however they choose.

This is a challenge, but an exciting one. A website flattens hierarchies and processes, and makes it hard to communicate different periods in one's work. Do you make the left–hand column chronological? Will 'current' and 'past' communicate the interval between, say, art school work and a first, large public commission? The uniformity of these platforms makes it hard to draw distinctions. As a response to these concerns, a number of artists have sites that feature no images. But art means engaging with images. The visual literacy we learn by looking at contemporary art can be translated to the way we think through images via different media. It can exemplify and help us to recognise that authority is asserted visually. But from that sense of authority we could deduce the power of disengaging. That to opt out of the primacy of the image could also be a point of strength, and enable greater control over the presentation of one's work.

The artist's website is not net art. Nor is it a Tumblr – though many artists use the microblogging platform in lieu of or in addition to their websites, allowing for a different form of engagement with the flow of imagery online that almost negates many of the claims of this essay (except a central one: Tumblr is a uniform platform, except for the 'themes' that allow customisation, not different from Cargo's design templates) since Tumblr has created an architecture of aggregation, organisation and recirculation of images that is coherent and at times exciting. In comparison, Indexhibit, Cargo, and Wordpress seem like easy victims. The moving parts of an artist's website as delineated above – CV, contact, images, text – are the information a visitor is looking for. Why chip away at established structures, especially ones developed to relay specific types of knowledge? Why not instead discuss the uniformity of gallery websites or the crimes that are most major art magazines' websites? Wouldn't it be better to dedicate the time to thinking through the presentation of contemporary art in online exhibition spaces?

The answer to all of the above is that while we think we see a lot of art online, we are lost in a sea of images. Though seeing art onscreen has become habitual, there are still very few good online exhibition platforms, and none of them are as well-funded or as sustainable as your regular run-of-the mill European kunsthalle. The current moment is one of an audience without much to look at. We are miles away from the early 2000s, when museum visitors complained about being shown net art on a desktop in the gallery space since they sit at a computer all day long at work, but yards away from a healthy number of online exhibition spaces. One of the reasons for that is access: to start an online exhibition platform requires programming knowledge. It's a requirement not only in order to build such a platform, but also simply to be able to imagine what is possible when working online. The latter goes for both the artist and the curator working online. Those online exhibition platforms and commissioning organisations that do exist are doing important work in enhancing visitors' understanding of what could be done online, stepping away at great pace from the blogroll of installation shots. But rarely do they facilitate access to the non-tech-savvy, be they artists who may want to work with them or viewers trying to understand the technique.

4.

Indexhibit's homepage shows a list of words slowly emerging on the screen. It's almost impossible to filter the ones which best reflect the ethos of the content management system. A selection will be insufficient:

> Alternative Anti-Establishment Archetypal Bohemian Collaborative Committed
> Conceptual Connected Constant Default Democratic Functional Happy Idiosyncratic
> Independent Irregular Grassroots Long-Term Maverick Modernist Minimalist
> Networked Non-Conformist Original Organised Pioneering Punk Pragmatic
> Progressive Radical Reductive Revolutionary Self-Sufficient Seminal Social Ubiquitous
> Unapologetic Unorthodox Universal Utilitarian Zen

From 'alternative' to 'utilitarian zen' (hello, new-age neologism!), the artist's website is the patchwork result of many different needs, from a digital business card to an online portfolio and digital archive. But could it be more?

A precursor or role model for a new form and use for the artist's website could be the artist's book. Often printed in small editions, artist-made publications date back to illuminated manuscripts in medieval times, but reached their peak in the twentieth century, parallel to the mass production and availability of books. The artist's book confronted similar temptations to those we now see on the internet: uniformity of design, the notion that the work of art circulates in a much wider network than it would in an exhibition space, and a sense that more could be done within the structures of a known format. An artist's book is not a catalogue. Maybe the artist's website could be the same: an updating site exhibiting works in a considered manner that responds to the possibilities the web offers. It could be a place to experiment, to try out ideas, and to connect with viewers. Such a website will generate an engagement rare at the moment: visitors might tune in periodically to see what's on view, just as they would step into a familiar gallery.

The lasting form of artists' books will continue to be an example for production related to digital technology, as we are seeing a growing number of artworks that use two hybridised book/digital forms: the e-book and print-on-demand. Both could also step into the void left by portfolios. A catalogue raisonné – an established print product compiling the entirety of an artist's production – for a living artist is infinitely more usable as an updating e-book platform than in print (not to mention many of these books span numerous, massive volumes complete with often poor reproductions), leaving the website to be a living, current space for experimentation with the presentation of work.

To maintain a website is labour, yet another item in the artist's lengthy digital to-do list after other non-artmaking professionalised activities like replying to emails and maintaining a social media presence. Arguably, the personal website is more important than social media platforms (though not, of course, than email, which is the face of work today), since at least its structure – not its distribution – is independent of the platforms of huge corporations like Facebook/Instagram, Tumblr/Yahoo!, or Google. The fact that contemporary artists are spread thin doing work outside their actual practice – and that's without counting the endless applications to residencies, fellowships, awards, and so on that define much of the artist–statement– inflected practice that the contemporary art world demands – may be discouraging, but shouldn't deter any artist from thinking through what it means to maintain a web– site and how, instead of a bland showroom, theirs could be a fresh exhibition space.

There is no way to undo the current proliferation of images. Nor should we want to: the contemporary state of hyper image literacy informs the work of artists, curators and critics just as much as it does the viewing of their work by the public. But maybe we can look to artists to challenge how we look at images – and art – today.

THE MOST IMPORTANT THING IS TO ENJOY YOURSELF AND HAVE A GOOD TIME

BY

ALEXANDRA KLEEMAN

OF ALL OF THEM, AMANDA MICHAELS is the only one I can remember as she was before the party, swinging her stringy yellow hair as she leans forward into her desk to get my attention. She holds a piece of notebook paper folded over many times. *Read and eat*, she hisses, meaning there is something written inside that is so dangerous it ought to be destroyed. I unfold it, swivel all the way around in my seat to find her gaze. With our eyes locked, I open my mouth. I crush the note in my palm and push it into my hole, chewing hard. It tastes sour, dry, salty from the touch of teen-age hands. Amanda's lips mouth the word over and over again, silently: *Party. Party. Party. Party.* Her petite hand a petite fist. But these days she barely knows who I am.

We hated inevitable change, but we liked this kind of change. I watched the other girls grow beautiful right before my eyes. Breasts swell on their bodies like flowers blooming in time-lapse. They hold the bottles vertical and let the beer fall straight down their throats, hair blown back by a breeze from nowhere, skin gleaming with predatory clarity. In the light of somebody's dad's old green banker's lamp, a boy takes the horn-rimmed glasses off Wendy Jenkins' face and like black magic we see her perfect nose for the first time, foxy as hell. Covering my own nose with one hand, I cheer with the others for Wendy and the brand new face she'd always had. The boys chug and their throats pulse with drinking, as though they had huge hearts, hurtling blood. They feel sexy and it makes them sexy. When anybody tells a joke they erupt, spew pinkish mist. Everything is funny to them.

We snort Smirnoff and Jägermeister from the pits of our sticky palms, mix jug whiskey with generic cola, pick colourful pills off the sparkle-bombed counters and lay them upon the hungry pink of our tongues. Everywhere I look, there we are: writhing on coffee tables and couches, slick with sweat and sucking face. Everyone is becoming their best self right in front of me! And even if I haven't been trans-formed yet, I know there's something new lodged in me: a pang of omnipotence when I kneel at the base of the vodka luge, mouth open to receive *whatever*. Like a mother feels when her baby kicks inside of her for the first time, but with no mother and no baby. As something burns inside my nose, I climb on top of the foosball table to show Amanda Michaels who I've become. *PARTY MONSTER*, I yell into the packed, swaying room. Amanda's in the corner, trawling the mouth of some guy with a buzzcut. Without pausing, she turns her eyes up toward me and gives the double thumbs-up.

We party, we sleep, we party. We live in a never-ending present tense. We sleep on moist carpet with popcorn in our hair and glitter in our spit. Our hair grows shaggy, we hold it taut and cut at it with knives made for steak. Days pass faster, with-out texture or shape, and still the party fails to end. Is it that we can't stop, or that we won't? Waking with mouths tasting rotten and sweet, among limbs and bottles and potato chip dust, lying there in the dark until somebody gets up to plug in the twinkle lights. Daylight comes in bursts now – twenty-five minutes, thirty minutes, less each day – and we fall into concussive slumber. We sit up reaching for the nearest cup and go to fill it. Now when I look around the room I see grown-up bodies poking out of the crop tops, thick, matted hair seeping out from the waistband of cargo shorts. They've changed, in ways both qualitative and quantitative: around their mouths are blurry patches, dark lines, they don't have the usual number of teeth. I reach up to feel my own mouth, and find that I'm not smiling at all.

Never-ending means forever. *We'll run out of food*, I say, but we never do. *We'll run out of water*, I say, but we never need it. Devin Eccleston crushes an aluminium can against his forehead. Katie Mitchell barfs into the dank basin of a potted palm. Trevor with the tiger tattoo sags in the corner, he hasn't moved for weeks. I drape a stray T-shirt over his face for privacy, and now his head reads JUST DO IT, with the sporty swoosh. It feels like a message from the universe, but it's so vague and so imperative. Suddenly I'm wiping the tears from my face, bountiful, overflowing, sloppy tears like beer in a beer commercial. *Who invited you?* asks a voice to my right. It's Amanda Michaels, squinting at me like I'm the fine print on a prescription pill bottle. *You did*, I answer. She looks confused for a moment. *That was forever ago*, she says, shrugging it off and wandering off toward the beer pong. But later on, Amanda's forgotten that she's mad at me. She saunters over in her stonewashed slim-fits, smoking a cigarette. She slings an arm around my neck, pulls me toward her. *Wooooooo!* she shouts. *Wooooooo*, I say back. I want to tell her *don't leave me* but she's already left. I watch as she walks over to another girl and does the exact same thing, and another, and another.

Sometimes I tell everyone I'm going to look for the bathroom, but instead I go to the back of the house where the party isn't raging so hard, where it's almost just a house. I walk down the hall trying each locked door. Every once in a while a doorknob turns in my hand and I push the door open to find the bedroom of a young girl, strange to me but familiar in the sense that I know I was one forever ago. The air inside is stale, the bed smells of fake flowers, has a fake softness. I pull the pillow up from under the covers and clutch it to my chest like it is a person I am in love with. I'm rocking back and forth, eyes closed, pretending to myself that I am very old and very mature, a college graduate, the owner of a practical, German-made automobile leased at a low interest rate. I imagine myself wearing a clean grey blazer and wool-blend skirt, spinning slow circles in an ergonomic office chair. If I really try, I can imagine a husband, standing with his back to me, facing the TV. He's standing with the remote control, flipping through the channels, looking for something I can't offer. I can't see his face. That's the type of person I want for my future: a stranger.

Sometimes, in the utter quiet of someone else's bedroom, I believe the person I'm imagining is out there somewhere, dressed in shades of putty in her studio apartment with nothing on the walls. She's clutching a pillow to her chest at night and dreaming of my life, where when all the cups are broken or dirty we lap liquid from the crook of an elbow or hollow of a navel, where the party never slows or stops or shrinks and is so large that it edges everything else out of your mind. *Save me from the dull times*, she says out loud to nobody. *Save me from becoming myself*. It is only through her eyes, which don't exist, that I see myself as the party wants me to see. Shiny. Rubbery. Laughing. I exit the bedroom with renewed self-envy, remembering that the most important thing is to enjoy yourself and have a good time. I enter the party over and over and over again. I exit the bedroom and enter the party. This is the life of our time.

SPONSORS

ONE DAY IN THE CITY:
27TH MAY 2016
UCL FESTIVAL OF CULTURE

"One Day in the City" is a bi-annual celebration of London communities and literary culture, through a variety of talks, performances, and pop-ups. The events are free to the public and take place in and around UCL's Bloomsbury Campus. Please do come along and join in the festivities.

The day opens with a debate, led by Andrew O'Hagan, on the contemporary novel and literary journalism.

There will be an informal reading and discussion of T.S. Eliot's "The Waste Land" by contemporary poets and members of the UCL community.

Peter Gizzi and Sarah Howe will give readings of their poetry, followed by Q&A.

John Lanchester and Jonathan Coe will discuss the state-of-the-nation novel.

Tom McCarthy will be in conversation, discussing "Space, Data, and the Death Drive".

For more information follow us:
twitter:@onedayinthecity
facebook: https://www.facebook.com/onedayinthecity
email: n.shepley@ucl.ac.uk

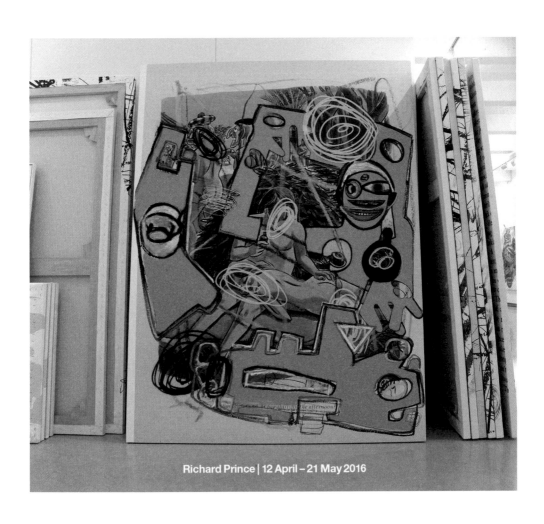

Richard Prince | 12 April – 21 May 2016

Tuesday–Saturday 11–6
62 Kingly Street
London W1B 5QN
www.sadiecoles.com

Sadie Coles   HQ

Current and forthcoming with Fitzcarraldo Editions

2014
Zone by Mathias Enard
Memory Theatre by Simon Critchley

2015
On Immunity by Eula Biss
My Documents by Alejandro Zambra
It's No Good by Kirill Medvedev
Street of Thieves by Mathias Enard
Notes on Suicide by Simon Critchley
Pond by Claire-Louise Bennett
Nicotine by Gregor Hens
Nocilla Dream by Agustín Fernández Mallo

2016
Pretentiousness: Why it Matters by Dan Fox
Counternarratives by John Keene
Football by Jean-Philippe Toussaint
Second-hand Time by Svetlana Alexievich
The Hatred of Poetry by Ben Lerner
The Doll's Alphabet by Camilla Grudova
A Primer for Cadavers by Ed Atkins
Bricks and Mortar by Clemens Meyer

Fitzcarraldo Editions

For more information please visit fitzcarraldoeditions.com

London Review
OF BOOKS

Subscribe Now

12 issues for £12

Connect with the world's most entertaining writers and critics

Subscribe today and you will receive:
- The *London Review of Books* magazine delivered direct to your door
- FREE unfettered access to the searchable online digital archive
- The latest issues FREE on your iPad, iPhone or Android device through the LRB app, so you can take the LRB everywhere you go

Subscribe now to become part of the conversation.

www.mylrb.co.uk/nsoffer

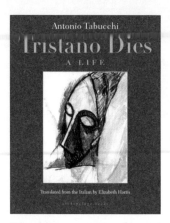

In Ikonomou's concrete streets, the rain is always looming... Yet even at the edge of destitution, his men and women act for themselves, trying to preserve what little solidarity remains in a deeply atomized society... There is faith here, deep faith – though little or none in those who habitually ask for it.
MARK MAZOWER, *The Nation*

Tabucchi's prose creates a deep and sometimes heart-wrenching nostalgia and constantly evokes the pain of recognizing the speed of life's passing which everyone knows but few have the strength to accept... Wonderfully thought-provoking and beautiful.
ALAN CHEUSE,
NPR's All Things Considered

Halfway between fairy tale and science fiction, between religious and sacreligious, between poetry and philosophy, this book looks with careful but compelling insistence at the mystery of what happens in "the dark funnel" of a life.
ANNA RUCHAT, *Pulp*

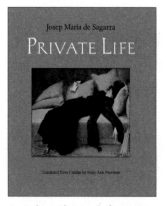

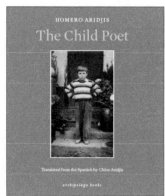

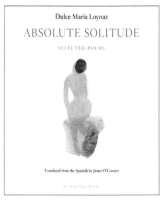

A graphic and viciously funny Catalan social satire . . . This is a risqué novel, sustained by humour and a sleazy elegance, all steeped in ironies.
EILEEN BATTERSBY,
The Irish Times

The poetry of Homero Aridjis is a symbol of love. His work is very beautiful, above all, his style is very original, very novel.
JUAN RULFO

Archaic and new, a phosphorescent reality of her own incredibly human poetry, her fresh language, tender, weightless, rich in abandon, in feeling, the mystic irony on the lined paper of her everyday notebook like roses shrouded in the common
JUAN RAMÓN JIMÉNEZ

 archipelago books

www.archipelagobooks.org • www.facebook.com/archipelagobooks • www.twitter.com/archipelagobks

Art Monthly

contemporary visual art magazine
Taking art apart since 1976

**Special offer for
White Review readers**

Subscribe to the print edition
and receive a free digital
subscription with full online
access to the entire
Art Monthly back catalogue
of 400 issues.

www.artmonthly.co.uk/whitereview2016
offer ends 15 July 2016

THE WHITE REVIEW

SUBSCRIBE!

20 per cent off all back issues, using the code BASICNEEDS
Offer expires 15 July 2016
www.thewhitereview.org

APPENDIX

MICHAEL BARRON has written for *HARPER'S*, *BOMB MAGAZINE*, *VICE*, and *PITCHFORK*. He lives in Brooklyn.

AMY BESSONE was born in The Bronx, NY in 1970 and studied in Paris and Amsterdam. After working for many years in Brussels, Belgium she moved to Los Angeles, CA in 2004. She lives in the Hollywood Hills with her two children and a cockapoo named Prinzessin von Heinstein. Bessone's ceramic torsos were made with the support of the Cal State University Long Beach Ceramics Department and have been shown at Salon 94, New York (2015) and Gavlak, Los Angeles (2016). In collaboration with super producer Butch Vig, Bessone is currently working on her first hip–hop album under her rap name BessoneBOT.

NICHOLAS CULLINAN is the director of the National Portrait Gallery.

TRISTAN GARCIA was born in 1981 in Toulouse. His début novel, *HATE: A ROMANCE* (Faber and Faber, 2010), was a critical success and won the Prix de Flore in 2008. A philosopher by training, he completed his PhD and published *FORM AND OBJECT. A TREATISE ON THINGS* (Edinburgh University Press, 2014) even as he continued to write fiction prolifically. 'Walking Backwards' is a story from his most recent book, 7.

ORIT GAT is a writer based in New York and London whose work on art, publishing, and internet culture has appeared in a variety of magazines. She is the features editor of *RHIZOME* and was recently awarded the Creative Capital/Andy Warhol Arts Writers Grant.

LAWRENCE ABU HAMDAN has made projects in the form of audiovisual installations, performances, graphic works, photography, Islamic sermons, cassette tape com-positions, potato chip packets, essays, and lectures. In 2013 his audio documentary *THE FREEDOM OF SPEECH ITSELF* was submitted as evidence at the UK asylum tribunal and the artist called to testify as an expert witness. He continues to make sonic analyses for legal investigations and advocacy. His works are part of collections at MoMA New York, Van AbbeMuseum Eindhoven and the Arts Council, England. This transcript was originally published in the artist's book *[INAUDIBLE] A POLITICS OF LISTENING IN 4 ACTS* published on the occasion of the exhibition *EARSHOT* at Portikus Frankfurt, 2016. Translation by Masha Refka. Transcription by Masha Refka & Lawrence Abu Hamdan.

EVAN HARRIS writes fiction, essays and poetry, and has been published by *The White Review*, *OpenDemocracy*, *Litro*, *3AM: Magazine*, *Ink Sweat and Tears*, *Metazen*, and *The Quietus*. He has taught English in London, Bishkek and Budapest, and worked as a freelance editor and reader.

ALICE HATTRICK is a writer and producer based in London. She is currently contributing editor of *EROS* journal and co-editor of *Aorist* magazine.

ALEXANDRA KLEEMAN is a writer based in New York. Her debut novel *You Too Can Have A Body Like Mine* was published by Harper in 2015 and she is the winner of the 2016 Bard Fiction Prize. Her fiction has been published in *The Paris Review*, *Zoetrope: All-Story*, *Conjunctions*, *Guernica*, and *Gulf Coast*, among others. Non-fiction essays and reportage have appeared in *Harper's*, *Tin House*, *n+1*, and the *Guardian*. Her work has received scholarships and grants from Bread Loaf, the Virginia Center for the Creative Arts, Santa Fe Art Institute, and ArtFarm Nebraska. A collection of short stories, *Intimations*, is forthcoming by Harper in September 2016.

CHRIS KRAUS is the author of four novels, *I Love Dick* (Semiotexte, 1997), *Aliens & Anorexia* (Semiotexte, 2000), *Torpor* (Semiotexte, 2006) and *Summer of Hate* (Semiotexte, 2012), and two books of cultural criticism, *Video Green* (Semiotexte, 2004) and *Where Art Belongs* (Semiotexte, 2011). She was born in New York and raised in New Zealand. She teaches creative writing at The European Graduate School in Switzerland. She lives in LA.

MARTIN MACINNES was born in Inverness in 1983. He has an MA from the University of York, has read at international science and literature festivals, and is the winner of a Scottish Book Trust New Writers Award and the 2014 Manchester Fiction Prize. His novel *Infinite Ground*, from which 'Flying to the Interior' is excerpted, is forthcoming from Atlantic Books in August 2016.

GEOFFREY G. O'BRIEN is an American poet, author of several collections including *People on Sunday* (Wave Books, 2013), *Metropole* (UCP, 2011), *Green and Gray* (UCP, 2007), and *The Guns and Flags Project* (UCP, 2002). O'Brien has taught at the University of California, Berkeley, and for San Quentin State Prison's Prison University Project. He lives in California.

EILEEN QUINLAN was born in 1972 in Boston. She lives and works in New York. She received her MFA from Columbia University, New York (2005). Her work is included in the public collections of MoMA, New York, the Whitney Museum of American Art, New York, Los Angeles County Museum of Art, The Museum of Contemporary Art, Los Angeles, The Metropolitan Museum of Art, New York, Seattle Art Museum, and FRAC (Fonds Regional d'Art Contemporain), France. Her work is currently on view at the Museum of Cycladic Art, Athens. Quinlan had a two-person exhibition at The Kitchen, New York in 2012 and a solo exhibition at the ICA in Boston in 2009. Past group exhibitions include *IMAGE SUPPORT* at Bergen Kunsthall, Norway (2016), *NEW PHOTOGRAPHY 2013*, curated by Roxana Marcoci at MoMA, New York, *RITES OF SPRING* at the Contemporary Arts Museum, Houston (2014), *WHAT IS A PHOTOGRAPH* at the International Center of Photography, New York (2014), and *ALL OF THIS AND NOTHING* at Hammer Museum, Los Angeles (2011).

SOPHIE SEITA's published works include *MEAT* (Little Red Leaves, 2015), *12 STEPS* (Wide Range, 2012), *FANTASIAS IN COUNTING* (BlazeVOX, 2014) and *I MEAN I DISLIKE THAT FATE THAT I WAS MADE TO WHERE*, a translation of the German poet Uljana Wolf (Wonder, 2015). She is the recipient of the John Kinsella and Tracy Ryan Poetry Prize (2012), the second Wonder Book Prize (2014, with Uljana Wolf), and the recipient of a PEN/Heim Award (2015) for her forthcoming full-length translation of *SUBSISTERS: SELECTED POEMS* by Uljana Wolf (Belladonna, 2016).

MICHAEL WOLF's photography documents the architecture and the vernacular culture of metropolises. He grew up in Canada, Europe and the United States, studying at UC Berkeley and at the Folkwang School with Otto Steinert in Essen, Germany. He moved to Hong Kong in 1994 where he worked for 8 years as contract photographer for *STERN* magazine. Since 2001, Wolf has been focusing on his own projects, many of which have been published as books. More of his work can be seen at www.photomichaelwolf.com.

JEFFREY ZUCKERMAN is Digital Editor at *MUSIC & LITERATURE* magazine and a translator from French. He has served on the 2016 jury for the PEN Translation Prize, and is currently translating Ananda Devi's *EVE OUT OF HER RUINS* (Deep Vellum, 2016) and Antoine Volodine's *RADIANT TERMINUS* (Open Letter, 2017). His writing and translations have appeared in *BEST EUROPEAN FICTION*, the *LOS ANGELES REVIEW OF BOOKS*, the *PARIS REVIEW DAILY*, the *NEW REPUBLIC*, and *VICE*. In his free time, he does not listen to music.

FRIENDS OF THE WHITE REVIEW

AARON BOGART

ABI MITCHELL

ABIGAIL YUE WANG

ADAM FREUDENHEIM

ADAM HALL

ADAM SAUNBY

ADELINE DE MONSEIGNAT

AGRI ISMAIL

AJ DEHANY

ALAN MURRIN

ALBA ZIEGLER–BAILEY

ALBERT BUCHARD

ALEX GREINER

ALEX MCDONALD

ALEX MCELROY

ALEXA MITTERHUBER

ALICE OSWALD

ALIX MCCAFFREY

AMBIKA SUBRAMANIAM

AMI GREKO

AMY SHERLOCK

ANASTASIA SVOBODA

ANASTASIA VIKHORNOVA

AND OTHER STORIES

ANDREW CURRAN

ANDREW LELAND

ANDREW ROADS

ANNA DELLA SUBIN

ANNA WHITE

ANNE MEADOWS

ANNE WALTON

ARCHIPELAGO BOOKS

ARIANNE LOVELACE

ARIKE OKE

ASIA LITERARY AGENCY

AUDE FOURGOUS

BAPTISTE VANPOULLE

BARBARA HORIUCHI

BARNEY WALSH

BEN HINSHAW

BEN LERNER

BEN POLLNER

BERNADETTE EASTHAM

BOOK/SHOP

BRIAN WILLIAMS

BRIGITTE HOLLWEG

BROOMBERG & CHANARIN

CAMILLE GAJEWSKI

CAMILLE HENROT

CARLOTTA EDEN

CAROL HUSTON

CAROLINE LANGLEY

CAROLINE YOUNGER

CAROLYN LEK

CARRIE ETTER

CATHERINE HAMILTON

CERI JANE WEIGHTMAN

CHARLES LUTYENS

CHARLIE HARKIN

CHARLOTTE COHEN

CHARLOTTE GRACE

CHEE LUP WAN

CHINA MIÉVILLE

CHISENHALE GALLERY

CHRIS KRAUS

CHRIS WEBB

CHRISTIAN LORENTZEN

CHRISTOPHER GRAY

CJ CAREY

CLAIRE DE DIVONNE

CLAIRE DE ROUEN

CLAIRE–LOUISE BENNETT

CLAUDE ADJIL

CODY STUART

CONOR DELAHUNTY

COSMO LANDESMAN

CRISTOBAL BIANCHI

CYNTHIA & WILLIAM MORRISON–BELL

CYRILLE GONZALVES

DANIEL COHEN

DANIELA BECHLY

DANIELA SUN

DAVID AND HARRIET POWELL

DAVID ANDREW

DAVID BARNETT

DAVID BREUER

DAVID EASTHAM

DAVID ROSE

DAVID THORNE

DEBORAH LEVY

DEBORAH SMITH

DES LLOYD BEHARI

DEV KARAN AHUJA

DOUGLAS CANDANO

DR GEORGE HENSON

DR SAM NORTH

ED BROWNE

ED CUMMING

EDDIE REDMAYNE

EDWARD GRACE

ELEANOR CHANDLER

ELEY WILLIAMS

ELIAS FECHER

ELSPETH MITCHELL

EMILY BUTLER

EMILY LUTYENS

EMILY RUDGE

EMMA WARREN

ENRICO TASSI

EPILOGUE

EUAN MONAGHAN

EUGENIA LAPTEVA

EUROPA EDITIONS

EVA KELLENBERGER

FABER & FABER

FABER ACADEMY

FABER MEMBERS

FANNY SINGER

FATOS USTEK

FIONA GEILINGER

FIONA GRADY

FITZCARRALDO EDITIONS

FLORA CADZOW

FOLIO SOCIETY

FOUR CORNERS BOOKS

FRANCESCO PEDRAGLIO

GABRIEL VOGT

GALLAGHER LAWSON

GARY HABER

GEORGE HICKS

GEORGETTE TESTARD

GEORGIA GRIFFITHS

GEORGIA LANGLEY

GERMAN SIERRA

GHISLAIN DE RINCQUESEN

GILDA WILLIAMS

GILLIAN GRANT

GLENN BURTON

GRANTA BOOKS

HANNAH BARRY

HANNAH NAGLE

HANNAH WESTLAND

HANS ULRICH OBRIST

HARRIET HOROBIN–WORLEY

HARRY ECCLES–WILLIAMS

HARRY VAN DE BOSPOORT

HATTIE FOSTER

HAYLEY DIXON

HEADMASTER MAGAZINE

HELEN BARRELL

HELEN PYE

HELEN THORNE

HEMAN CHONG

HENRIETTTA SPIEGELBERG

HENRY HARDING

HENRY MARTIN

HENRY WRIGHT

HIKARI YOKOYAMA

HONEY LUARD

HORATIA HARROD

HOW TO ACADEMY

IAIN BROOME

IAN CHUNG

ICA

ISELIN SKOGLI

JACOB GARDNER

JACQUES STRAUSS

JADE FRENCH

JADE KOCH

JAMES BROOKES

JAMES KING

JAMES MEWIS

JAMES PUSEY

JAMES TURNBULL

JASPER ZAGAET

JAYA PRADHAN

JEANNE CONSTANS

JENNIFER CUSTER

JENNIFER HAMILTON–EMERY

JEREMY ADDISON

JEREMY DELLER

JEREMY MOULTON

JES FERNIE

JESSICA CRAIG

JESSICA SANTASCOY

JIAN WEI LIM

JO COLLEY

JOANNA WALSH

JOHN GORDON

JOHN LANGLEY

JOHN MURRAY

JOHN SCANLAN

JOHN SCHANCK

JOHN SIMNETT

JON DAY

FRIENDS OF THE WHITE REVIEW

JONATHAN CAPE
JONATHAN DUNCAN
JONATHAN WILLIAMS
JORDAN BASS
JORDAN HUMPHREYS
JORDAN RAZAVI
JORDI CARLES SUBIRA
JOSEPH DE LACEY
JOSEPH EDWARD
JOSEPHINE NEW
JOSHUA COHEN
JOSHUA DAVIS
JUDY BIRKBECK
JULIA CRABTREE
JULIA DINAN
JULIE PACHICO
JULIEN BÉZILLE
JURATE GACIONYTE
JUSTIN JAMES WALSH
KAJA MURAWSKA
KAMIYE FURUTA
KATE BRIGGS
KATE LOFTUS-O'BRIEN
KATE WILLS
KATHERINE LOCKTON
KATHERINE RUNDELL
KATHERINE TEMPLAR LEWIS
KATHRYN MARIS
KATHRYN SIEGEL
KEENAN MCCRACKEN
KIERAN CLANCY
KIERAN RID
KIRSTEEN HARDIE
KIT BUCHAN
KYLE PARKER
LAURA SNOAD
LAUREN ELKIN
LEAH SWAIN
LEE JORDAN
LEON DISCHE BECKER
LEWIS BUNGENER
LIA TEN BRINK
LIAM ROGERS
LILI HAMLYN
LILLIPUT PRESS
L'IMPOSSIBLE
LITERARY KITCHEN
LORENZ KLINGEBIEL
LOUISE GUINNESS
LOZANA ROSSENOVA
LUCIA PIETROIUSTI
LUCIE ELVEN
LUCY KUMARA MOORE
LUISA DE LANCASTRE
LUIZA SAUMA
MACK
MACLEHOSE PRESS
MAJDA GAMA
MALTE KOSIAN
MARIA DIMITROVA
MARIANNA SIMNETT
MARILOU TESTARD
MARIS KREIZMAN
MARK EL-KHATIB
MARK KROTOV

MARKUS ZETT
MARTA ARENAL LLORENTE
MARTIN CREED
MARTIN NICHOLAS
MATHILDE CABANAS
MATT GOLD
MATT HURCOMB
MATT MASTRICOVA
MATTHEW BALL
MATTHEW JOHNSTON
MATTHEW PONSFORD
MATTHEW RUDMAN
MAX FARRAR
MAX PORTER
MAX YOUNGMAN
MAXIME DARGAUD-FONS
MEGAN PIPER
MELISSA GOLDBERG
MELVILLE HOUSE
MICHAEL GREENWOLD
MICHAEL HOLTMANN
MICHAEL LEUE
MICHAEL SIGNORELLI
MICHAEL TROUGHTON
MICHELE SNYDER
MILES JOHNSON
MINIMONIOTAKU
MIRIAM GORDIS
MONICA OLIVEIRA
MONICA TIMMS
NAOMI CHANNA
NATHAN BRYANT
NATHAN FRANCIS
NED BEAUMAN
NEDA NEYNSKA
NEIL D.A. STEWART
NEW DIRECTIONS
NICK MULGREW
NICK SKIDMORE
NICK VOSS
NICKY BEAVEN
NICOLA SMYTH
NICOLAS CHAUVIN
NICOLE SIBELET
NILLY VON BAIBUS
OLEKSIY OSNACH
OLGA GROTOVA
OLI JACOBS
OLIVER BASCIANO
OLIVIA HEAL
OLIVIER RICHON
ONEWORLD
ORLANDO WHITFIELD
OSCAR GAYNOR
OWEN BOOTH
ØYSTEIN W ARBO
PADDY KELLY
PANGAEA SCULPTORS CENTRE
PATRICK GODDARD
PATRICK HAMM
PATRICK RAMBAUD
PATRICK STAFF
PAUL KEEGAN
PAUL TEASDALE
PEDRO

PEIRENE PRESS
PENGUIN BOOKS
PETER MURRAY
PHILIBERT DE DIVONNE
PHILIP JAMES MAUGHAN
PHILLIP KIM
PHOEBE STUBBS
PICADOR
PIERRE TESTARD
PIERS BARCLAY
PRIMORDIAL SEA
PUSHKIN PRESS
RACHEL ANDREWS
RACHEL GRACE
REBECCA SERVADIO
RENATE PRANCANE
RENATUS WU
RHYS TIMSON
RICHARD GLUCKMAN
RICHARD WENTWORTH
ROB SHARP
ROB SHERWOOD
ROBERT O'MEARA
ROBIN CAMERON
ROC SANDFORD
RORY O'KEEFFE
ROSALIND FURNESS
ROSANNA BOSCAWEN
ROSE BARCLAY
ROSIE CLARKE
RUBY COWLING
RUPERT CABBELL MANNERS
RUPERT MARTIN
RYAN CHAPMAN
RYAN EYERS
SADIE SMITH
SALLY BAILEY
SALLY MERCER
SALVAGE MAGAZINE
SAM BROWN
SAM GORDON
SAM MOSS
SAM SOLNICK
SAM THORNE
SAMUEL HUNT
SANAM GHARAGOZLOU
SARA BURNS
SARAH HARDIE
SARAH Y. VARNAM
SASKIA VOGEL
SCOTT ESPOSITO
SEAN HOOD
SEB EASTHAM
SELF PUBLISH, BE HAPPY
SERPENTINE GALLERY
SERPENT'S TAIL
SHARMAINE LOVEGROVE
SHOOTER LITERARY MAGAZINE
SIMON HARPER
SIMON WILLIAMS
SIMONE SCHRÖDER
SJOERD KRUIKEMEIER
SK THALE
SKENDER GHILAGA
SOPHIE CUNDALE

FRIENDS OF THE WHITE REVIEW

SOUMEYA ROBERTS
SOUTH LONDON GALLERY
SPIKE ISLAND
STEFANOS KOKOTOS
STEPHANIE TURNER
STEVE FLETCHER
SUSAN TOMASELLI
TAYLOR LE MELLE
TED MARTIN GREIJER
TELMO PRODUCCIONES
TERRIN WINKEL
THE ALARMIST
THE APPROACH
THE LETTER PRESS
THE REAL MATT WRIGHT
THEA HAWLIN
THEA URDAL
THEMISTOKLIS GIOKROUSSIS
THIBAULT CABANAS
THOMAS BUNSTEAD
THOMAS FRANCIS
THOMAS MOHR
THREE STAR BOOKS
TIM CURTAIN
TIMOTHY RENNIE
TITOUAN RUSSO
TOM GRACE
TOM JONES
TOM MCCARTHY
TROLLEY BOOKS
TZE–WEN CHAO
VALERIE BONNARDEL
VANESSA NICHOLAS
VERONIQUE TESTARD
VERSO BOOKS
VICTORIA MCGEE
VICTORIA MIRO
VIKTOR TIMOFEEV
VITA PEACOCK
WAYNE DALY
WEFUND.CO.UK
WHITE CUBE
WILL
WILL CHANCELLOR
WILL HEYWARD
WILL PALLEY
WILL SELF
WILLIAM ALDERWICK
WILLIAM CAIRNS
WILLOW GOLD
YASMINE SEALE
ZAYNAB DENA ZIARI
ZOE PILGER
ZOYA ROUS